THE TUSCAN
TYCOON'S WIFE

THE TUSCAN TYCOON'S WIFE

BY

LUCY GORDON

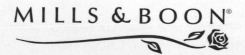

MILLS & BOON®

This book is dedicated to Janet Stover,
2001 World Champion Barrel Racer and Olympic Medalist,
who told me all about barrel racing and rodeos.

*First published in Great Britain 2003
Large Print edition 2003
Harlequin Mills & Boon Limited,
Eton House, 18-24 Paradise Road,
Richmond, Surrey TW9 1SR*

© *Lucy Gordon 2003*

ISBN 0 263 17960 5

*Set in Times Roman 16½ on 18½ pt.
16-1203-49812*

*Printed and bound in Great Britain
by Antony Rowe Ltd, Chippenham, Wiltshire*

CHAPTER ONE

'SELENA, you need either a miracle or a millionaire.'

Ben eased himself out from under the battered vehicle, monkey wrench in hand. He was lean, elderly, and had spent thirty years as a garage mechanic. Now those thirty years were telling him that Selena Gates wanted him to revive a corpse.

'This thing's had it,' he said gloomily surveying the van, which was actually a Mini Motor Home, with the accent on Mini.

'But you can make it go again?' Selena begged. 'I know you can, Ben. You're such a genius.'

'You stop that,' he said with an unconvincing attempt at severity. 'It doesn't work on me.'

'Always has so far,' she said, with perfect truth. 'You can make it go, can't you, Ben?'

'For a bit.'

'As far as Stephenville?'

'Three hundred miles? You don't want much! All right, it'll probably just about make it. But what then?'

'Then I'll win some money in the rodeo.'

'Riding that washed up brute?'

'Elliot is not washed up,' she flared. 'He's in his prime.'

Ben grunted. 'Been in his prime a few years, if you ask me.'

Any mention of her beloved Elliot touched a nerve, and Selena was about to defend him fiercely when she remembered that Ben, good friend that he was, was fixing her van on the cheap, and calmed down.

'Elliot and I will win something,' she said stubbornly.

'Enough for a new van?'

'Enough to get this one fixed as good as new.'

'Selena, there ain't enough money in the world to get this ramshackle old bus fixed as good as new. It was falling to bits when you bought it, and that was way back. You'd do better sweet-talking a millionaire into buying you a new van.'

'No point in me chasing a millionaire,' Selena sighed. 'Haven't got the figure for it.'

'Sez who?' Ben demanded loyally.

'Sez me!'

He regarded her tall, ultra-slim figure. 'Maybe you're a little flat-chested,' he admitted.

'Ben, under these old jeans I'm flat everything.' She grinned with rueful self-mockery. 'It's no use. Millionaires like their women—' with both hands she traced the outline of a voluptuous figure. 'And that's something I never was. Haven't got the hair for it either. You need long, wavy tresses not—' she pointed to her boyish crop.

It was a startling red that blazed out like a beacon, telling the world, 'I'm here!' There was no way to overlook Selena. Smart, cheeky, independent, and optimistic to the point of craziness, she was her own woman. Anyone who challenged that soon learned the other lesson of that red hair. *Beware!*

'Besides,' Selena said, coming to her clincher argument, 'I don't *like* millionaires. They're not real people.'

Ben scratched his head. 'They aren't?'

'No way,' Selena said, like someone articulating an article of faith. 'They have too much money.'

'Too much money is what you could do with right now. Or a miracle.'

'A miracle would be easier,' she said. 'And I'll find one. No—it'll find me.'

'Darn it, Selena, will you try to be a bit realistic?'

'What for? What good did being realistic ever do me? Life's more fun if you expect the best.'

'And when the best don't happen?'

'Then think of another best and expect that. Ben, I promise you, somewhere, somehow, a genuine twenty-four-carat miracle is heading my way.'

Leo Calvani stretched his legs as far as he could, which wasn't far. The flight from Rome to Atlanta took twelve hours, and he travelled first class because if you were six foot three, and forty-two inches of that was leg, you needed all the help you could get.

Normally he didn't consider himself a 'first class' kind of man. Wealthy, yes. Afford the best, no problem. But frills and fuss made him nervous. So did cities, and fine clothes. That's why he travelled in his oldest jeans and denim jacket, complete with scuffed shoes. It was his way of saying that 'first class' wasn't going to get him.

An elegant stewardess hovered over him as solicitously as if he didn't look like a hobo. 'Champagne, sir?'

He took a moment to relish her large blue eyes and seductively curved figure. It was an instinctive reaction, a tribute paid to every woman under fifty, and since he was a warm-hearted man he usually found something to enjoy.

'Sir?'

'I'm sorry?'

'Would you like some champagne?'

'Whisky would be better.'

'Of course, sir. We have—' she rattled off a list of expensive brands until Leo's eyes glazed.

'Just whisky,' he said, with a touch of desperation.

As he sipped the drink he yawned and wished the journey away. Eleven hours gone and the last was the worst because he'd run out of distractions. He'd watched the film, enjoyed two excellent meals and flirted with the lady sitting beside him.

She'd responded cheerfully, attracted by his handsome, blunt-featured face framed by dark-brown hair with a touch of curl, and the lusty gleam in his blue eyes. They'd enjoyed a pleasant hour or two until she fell asleep. After that he flirted with the air hostesses.

But for the moment he was alone, with only his thoughts of the coming visit to occupy him. A couple of weeks on the Four-Ten, Barton Hanworth's ranch near Stephenville, Texas, enjoying wide-open spaces, the outdoor life, riding, attending the nearby rodeo, was his idea of heaven.

At last the great jet was descending to Atlanta. Soon he'd be able to stretch his legs, even if only for a couple of hours before squeezing his protesting frame onto the connecting flight to Dallas.

Ben pared the bill to the bone because he was fond of Selena, and he knew her next few dollars would go on Elliot's welfare. Any cents left over would buy food for herself, and if there were none, she'd go without. He helped her hitch the horse trailer onto the back of the van, kissed her cheek for luck and watched as she eased her way carefully out of his yard. As she vanished he sent up a prayer to whichever deity watched over crazy young women who had nothing in the world but a horse, a clapped-out van, the heart of a lion and a bellyful of stubbornness.

By the time Leo boarded the connecting flight at Atlanta jet lag was catching up with him and he managed to doze until they touched down. As he unfolded his long body he vowed never to get on another aeroplane as long as he lived. He did that after every flight.

As he came out of Customs he heard a booming voice.

'Leo, you young rascal!'

Leo's face lit up at the sight of his friend advancing on him with open arms.

'Barton, you *old* rascal!'

The next moment the two men were pummelling each other joyfully.

Barton Hanworth was in his fifties, a large amiable man with grizzled hair and the start of a paunch that his height still disguised. His voice and his laugh were enormous. So were his car, his ranch and his heart.

Leo made sure to study the car. In the six weeks since this trip was planned he'd spoken to Barton several times on the telephone, and never once had his friend missed the chance to talk about his 'new baby'. It was the latest, the loveliest, the fastest. He didn't mention price, but Leo had checked it online, and it was the costliest.

So now he knew his duty, and lavished praise on the big, silver beauty, and was rewarded by Barton's beaming smile.

Since Leo travelled light it took barely a moment to load his few bags, and they were away on the two-hour journey to the ranch near Stephenville.

'How come you flew from Rome?' Barton said, his eyes on the road. 'I thought Pisa was closer for you.'

'I was in Rome for my cousin Marco's engagement party,' Leo said. 'Do you know him? I forget.'

Barton grunted. 'He was at your farm when I came to Italy two years back, and bought those horses of yours. What's she like?'

'Harriet?' A big grin broke over Leo's handsome face. 'I tell you, Barton, if she weren't my cousin's fiancée—well, she is, more's the pity.'

'So Marco drew the prize and he's hog-tied at last?'

'Yes, I think he is,' Leo said thoughtfully. 'But I'm not sure if he knows it yet. If you believe him, he's making a "suitable" marriage to the granddaughter of his mother's old friend, but there was something very odd about that party. I don't know what happened ex-

actly, but afterward Marco spent the night outside, sleeping on the ground. I went out for a
breather at dawn, and saw him. He didn't see
me, so I vanished.'

'No explanations?'

'He never said a word. You know, Marco's
last engagement got broken off in a way nobody ever talks about.'

'And you think this one'll be the same?'

'Could be. It depends on how soon he real-
ises he's crazy about Harriet.'

'What about your brother? Isn't he going the
same way?'

'Oh, Guido's got enough sense to know
when he's crazy. He's all right. Dulcie's perfect for him.'

'So that just leaves you on the loose?'
Barton said with a fat chuckle.

'On the loose and happy to stay that way.
They won't catch me.'

'That's what they all say, but look around.
Good men are going down like ninepins.'

'Barton, have you any idea how many
women there are in the world?' Leo demanded.
'And how few of them I've managed to meet

so far? A man should be broad-minded, ex-
pand his horizons.'

'You'll find ''the one'', in the end,' Barton
said.

'But I do, time and again. Then the next day
I find another one who is also ''the one''.
That's how I get short-changed.'

'You? Short-changed?' Barton guffawed.

'True, I swear it. Look at me, all alone. No
loving wife, no kids.' He sighed sorrowfully.
'You don't know what a tragedy it is for a man
to realise that nature has made him fickle.'

'Yeah, sure!'

This time they both laughed. Leo had a delightful laugh, full of sun and wine, lusty with
life. He was a man of the earth, who instinc-
tively sought the open air and the pleasures of
the senses. It was all there in his eyes, and in
his big, relaxed body. But above all it was
there in his laugh.

On the last lap to Stephenville Barton began
to yawn.

'It's enough to make a man cross-eyed to be
staring at a horse's ass for so long,' he said.

Just ahead of them was an ancient, shabby horse trailer, displaying a large equine rump. It had been there for some time.

'Plus I had to get up at some ungodly hour to be at the airport on time,' Barton added.

'Hey, I'm sorry. You should have told me.'

'Well, it wasn't just that. We were up late last night, celebrating your visit.'

'But I wasn't there.'

'Don't fret. We'll celebrate again tonight,' Barton said, adding, by way of explanation, 'this is Texas.'

'So I see,' Leo said, grinning. 'I'm already beginning to wonder if I can take the pace. I'd offer to drive, but after that flight I'm in a worse state than you.'

'Well, it's not much further,' Barton grunted. 'Which is lucky because whoever's driving that horse trailer can't be doing more than fifty. Let's step on it.'

'Better not,' Leo advised quickly. 'If you're tired—'

'The sooner we're there the better. Here we go.'

He pulled out behind the horse trailer and speeded up to pass it. Glancing out of his window Leo saw the trailer slide back past them, then the van in front. He had a glimpse of the driver, a young woman with short, bristly red hair. She glanced up briefly and saw him looking at her.

What happened next became a bone of contention between them. She always said he winked at her. He swore she'd winked at him first. She said no way! It was a trick of the light and he had windmills in his head. They never did settle it.

Then Barton put his foot down, and they left her behind.

'Did you see that?' Leo asked. 'She winked at me. Barton? *Barton*!'

'OK, OK, I was just resting my eyes for a moment. But maybe you'd better talk to me—you know, just—sort of—'

'Just sort of keep you awake. Well, I'm not sure that overtaking has left us any better off.' Leo said, observing the pick-up truck that was now just ahead of them, and which was being driven erratically, swerving from lane to lane.

Barton swung right, meaning to overtake again, but the truck swung at the same moment, blocking him so that he had to fall back. He tried once more and the truck swung out a second time, and then slowed abruptly.

'Barton!' Leo said urgently, for his friend hadn't reacted.

At last Barton's reflexes seemed to kick in. It was too late to slow down. Only a halt would avoid a collision now and he slammed on the brakes, stopping just in time.

The van behind them wasn't so lucky. From out of sight came a squeal of brakes, then a thump, a shudder that went right through the car, and finally a howl of rage and anguish.

The truck that had caused the trouble sped on its way, the driver oblivious. The two men leapt out and ran behind to inspect the damage. The sight that met their eyes appalled them.

There was an ugly dent in the back of Barton's pride and joy, which exactly mirrored one in the front of the van. At the rear of the van things were even worse. The sudden braking had caused the horse trailer to slew sideways and crash against the vehicle with a force that had dented them both. The trailer had half overturned and was leaning drunkenly against the van, while inside, the terrified animal was lashing out, completing the demolition. Leo could see flying hooves appearing through the widening holes, then retreating for more kicks.

The young woman with red hair was struggling to get the trailer upright, an impossible task, but she went at it with frantic strength.

'Don't do that,' Leo yelled. 'You'll get hurt.'

She turned on him. *'Stay out of it!'* Her forehead was bleeding.

'You're hurt,' he said. 'Let me help—'

'I said stay out of it. Haven't you done enough?'

'Hey, I wasn't driving, and anyway it wasn't our—'

'What do I care which of you was driving? You're all the same. You rush around in your flash cars as though you owned the road, and you could have killed Elliot.'

'Elliot?'

Another crash from inside the trailer answered his question. The next moment the door had given way and the horse, hooves flailing, leapt out and into the road. Leo and the young woman raced for his head, but he evaded them both and galloped away, straight across the highway. Without a second's hesitation she tore after him, dodging the oncoming traffic.

'Crazy woman!' Leo said violently, and took off after her.

More squeals, braking, curses, frustrated drivers bawling graphic descriptions of how they would like to alter Leo's personal attributes. He ignored them and sprinted madly after her.

Barton scratched his head, muttered, 'Crazy as each other,' and got out his mobile phone.

Luckily for his two pursuers Elliot was slightly hurt and unable to go fast. Unluckily for them he was determined not to be caught. What he couldn't manage in speed he made up for in cunning, turning this way and that until he vanished into a clump of trees.

'You go that way,' Leo roared, 'I'll go this way, and between us we'll head him off.'

But their best efforts were unable to persuade the horse. Selena nearly succeeded, calling his name so that he paused and looked back. But then he was off again, managing to dart between them and heading back the way he'd come.

'Oh, no!' Leo breathed. 'Not the highway.'

In a frighteningly short space of time the traffic was in sight again. Appalled at what he could imagine happening, Leo put on a burst of speed, commanding his long legs to do their stuff. They obliged and he just made it, seizing the bridle with two yards to spare.

Elliot eyed him warily, but with Leo's first soothing words something seemed to come over him. He'd never heard the words before, for they were Italian, but Leo had the voice of a man who loved horses, speaking a universal language of affection. Elliot's shivering abated and he stood still, nervous and confused, but willing to trust.

Selena noticed all this subconsciously while she covered the last few yards, and the easy conquering of her beloved Elliot did nothing to improve her temper. Nor did the expert way this man was examining the animal's fetlocks, running gentle hands over them and finally saying, 'I don't think it's more serious than a slight strain, but a vet will confirm it.'

A vet's bill, when she was already scraping the bottom of her financial barrel. Lest he suspect that she was verging on despair she turned away, brushing a hand fiercely across her eyes. When she turned back anger and accusation were in place like a visor.

'More than a slight strain,' she echoed bitterly. 'There needn't have been any strain if you hadn't braked so suddenly.'

'Excuse me, I didn't do anything because I wasn't driving,' Leo said, breathing hard after his exertions. 'That was my friend, and it wasn't his fault either. Try blaming the guy who slowed in front of *us*. Not that you can do that because he's long gone, but if there's any fairness in the world—hell, what would you know about fairness?'

'I know about my injured horse and my damaged van. I know they got that way because I had to slam on my brakes at the last minute—'

'Ah, yes, your brakes. I'd be very interested to see your brakes. I'll bet they'd really prove interesting.'

'So now you're trying to put the blame on me!'

'I'm just—'

'That's the oldest scam in the book and you should be ashamed to try it.'

'I—'

'I know your sort. You think "woman alone", must be helpless. Let's try it on, see if she scares easy.'

'It never crossed my mind that you scared easy,' Leo retorted with perfect truth. 'As for helpless, I've seen man-eating tigers who were more helpless.'

Barton had crossed the road and caught up with them.

'Hold on a minute, Leo—'

Leo was normally the most easygoing of men, but he had a Latin temper that could flare impressively when it got going. It was going now.

'We're here aren't we? So blame us. We're just convenient scapegoats and—and—' As always when his English failed him he fell back on his native language and for the next minute words poured out of him in an unstoppable stream.

'Darn it, Leo!' Barton roared at last. 'Will you stop being so excitable and—and *Italian*?'

'I just wanted to say what I feel,' Leo said.

'Well, you did that. So why don't we all calm down and get acquainted?'

He turned to the young woman and introduced himself in his easygoing way.

'Barton Hanworth, Four-Ten Ranch, just outside Stephenville, about five miles ahead.'

'Selena Gates. On my way to Stephenville.'

'Fine. We can get your—er—vehicle seen to when we're there, and a vet for your horse.'

Selena tore her hair. 'But how are we going to get there? Fly?'

'Nope. I just made a call and help is on its way now. While we're waiting for things to get sorted out you'll stay with us a day or so.'

'I will?'

'Where else?' he asked genially. 'If I landed you in this fix, it's for me to get you out.'

Selena shot a suspicious look at Leo. 'But *he* says it wasn't your fault.'

'Well, I may have reacted just a little too late,' Barton conceded, unable to meet Leo's eye. 'Fact is, if I'd slowed sooner—well anyway, you don't want to take any notice of what my friend here says.' He leaned towards her conspiratorially. 'He's a foreigner—talks funny.'

'Thanks Barton,' Leo grinned.

He was still giving most of his attention to Elliot, stroking the horse's nose and murmuring in a way that the animal seemed to find calming. Selena watched him, saying nothing, seeing everything.

Whatever orders Barton had given must have been to the point, because in a short time things started happening. A truck appeared, drawing a slant-load gooseneck trailer, bearing the logo of the Four-Ten Ranch, and large enough for three horses.

Gently Selena led Elliot up the ramp. He was clearly limping now.

'There'll be a vet and a doctor waiting when we get home,' Barton said. 'Now, you get in the car with us, and we'll be off.'

'Thanks but I'll stay with Elliot,' she said.

Barton frowned. 'It's against the law for you to do that. Oh, what the hell?' he retreated, seeing her stubborn expression. 'It's only five miles.'

'I have to stay with Elliot,' Selena explained. 'He'll be nervous in a new place without me. What about my van?'

'Don't you worry, that's being attached now,' Barton assured her.

'Elliot doesn't like going too fast,' she said quickly.

'I'll make sure the driver knows that. Leo, you coming?'

'No, I think I'll stay here,' he said.

'I don't need any help with Elliot,' Selena said quickly.

'It's not Elliot I'm thinking of. You took a nasty bump on the head, and you shouldn't be on your own.'

'I'm all right.'

Leo climbed into the trailer and stood, arms folded, looking stubborn.

'We can start the journey and get Elliot to a vet, or we can stand here talking until you give in. It's up to you.'

He pulled the door closed as he spoke. Selena glared but didn't argue further. She even allowed him to help her settle Elliot in one of the stalls.

She was angry with him, without being quite sure why. She knew he hadn't been driving, and Barton Hanworth, who had been driving, was making handsome amends. But her nerves were jangled, she'd had the fright of her life, and all her agitation seemed to be homing in on this man who had the nerve to order her about, and was now talking to her in much the same soothing voice he'd used to calm Elliot. Crime of crimes!

'We'll be there soon,' he said. 'You can get some proper treatment.'

'I don't need mollycoddling,' she said through gritted teeth.

'Well, I would if I'd had a crash like you did.'

'I guess some of us are just tougher than others,' she said grumpily.

He left it there. She looked ill and he reckoned she was entitled to her bad temper. When she turned away to Elliot he watched, observing with wonder how she'd switched from bawling him out to being gentle and tender with the animal.

He was a quarter horse, not beautiful but solid and showing signs of a hard life. From the way she rested her cheek against his nose it was clear that he was perfect in her eyes.

At first glance she too wasn't beautiful, except for her eyes which were large and green. Her skin had the peachy glow of health and outdoor living, and her face looked as though it might be engagingly mischievous at a better time. Also Leo's observant eyes had noticed her movements with pleasure. She was as slim as a lathe, not elegant but tough and wiry, yet she moved with the instinctive grace of a dancer.

He tried to see her marvellous eyes again, without being obvious about it. With eyes like that a woman didn't need anything else. They did it all for her.

'My name's Leo Calvani,' he said, offering his hand.

She took it, and he immediately sensed the strength he'd guessed was there. He tightened his fingers a little, seeking to know more, but she withdrew her hand at once, having left it in his for no more than the minimum that courtesy demanded.

They started to move, slowly as Selena had insisted. After a few minutes he realised that she was studying him with curiosity. Not erotic curiosity, as he was used to. Or romantic fascination, which also came his way satisfyingly often.

Just curiosity. As though maybe he wasn't as bad as she'd first thought, and she was prepared to make allowances.

But no more than that.

CHAPTER TWO

THE Four-Ten Ranch was ten thousand acres of prime land, populated by five thousand head of cattle, two hundred horses, fifty employees and a family of six.

Selena knew she was in the presence of very serious money when she climbed stiffly out of the horse trailer and saw the stables where Barton kept his prize horseflesh. She knew humans who lived worse.

Everything moved like clockwork. As she walked in, leading Elliot, a man was pulling open the door of a large, comfortable stall. A vet was already there. So was a doctor, who would have drawn her aside, but Leo Calvani forestalled him with the quiet words, 'Let her attend the horse first. She won't settle down until she's seen him OK.'

She gave him a brief look of gratitude for his understanding, and watched jealously as the vet passed expert hands over Elliot and gave a diagnosis that was roughly the same as

30

Leo's, with a little elaboration to justify his fee. An anti-inflammatory injection, some bandaging, and it was over.

'Will he be fit for the rodeo next week?' Selena asked anxiously.

'We'll see. He's not a young horse any more.'

'How about letting the doctor look at you now?' Leo asked her.

She nodded and sat while the doctor examined her head. Beneath her apparent calm she was fighting despair. Her head was aching, her heart was aching and she was aching all over.

'How are those animals I sold you two years back?' Leo asked Barton. 'Shaping up?'

'Come and see for yourself.'

Together the two men walked along the stalls, and long, intelligent faces turned to watch them go by.

The five horses Barton had bought from Leo were in beautiful condition. They were large beasts with powerful hocks, and they'd been worked hard but treated like royalty.

'I'll swear they remember you,' Barton said as they nuzzled Leo.

'They don't forget a sucker.' Leo grinned.

While admiring the horses he contrived to glance at Selena, who was having a dressing fixed to her forehead.

'Take it easy for a day or two,' the doctor was saying. 'Plenty of rest.'

'It was just a little bump,' she insisted.

'Just a little bump on your head.'

'I'll make sure she rests,' Barton said. 'My wife's getting a room ready right now.'

'That's nice of her,' Selena said awkwardly, 'but I'd rather stay here with Elliot.'

She indicated the piles of hay as though wondering why anyone could want more.

'Well, you've gotta come in to eat,' Barton exclaimed. 'We're just having a snack because we'll be starting the barbecue in a couple of hours.'

'You're very kind but I can't come in the house,' Selena said, horribly conscious of her shabby, dishevelled appearance.

Barton scratched his head. 'Mrs Hanworth will be offended if you don't.'

'Then I'll come in and say thank you.'

She wouldn't need to stay long, she reckoned: just enough to be polite.

Reluctantly she followed them across to the house, which was a huge white mansion, the very sight of which made her feel awkward. She wondered how Leo would cope. In his shabby jeans and scuffed trainers he looked as out of place as she felt, although it didn't seem to bother him.

The sound of eager shrieks made Leo look up, and the next moment he was engulfed by the Hanworth family.

Delia, Barton's wife, was colourful, exuberant, and looked ten years younger than her true age. She and Barton had three children, two daughters, Carrie and Billie, younger versions of their mother, plus Jack, a studious son who seemed to live in a dream world, semi-detached from the rest of the family.

The household was completed by Paul, or Paulie as Delia insisted on calling him. He was her son by an earlier marriage, and the apple of her eye. She spoiled him absurdly, to the groaning exasperation of everyone else.

Paulie greeted Leo as a kindred spirit, slapping him on the back and predicting 'great times' together, which made Leo feel like groaning too. Paulie was in his late twenties,

good-looking in a fleshy, superficial way, but
self-indulgence was already blurring his fea-
tures. He was a businessman in his own esti-
mation, but his 'business' consisted of an internet company, his fifth, which was rapidly
failing, as the other four had failed.

Barton had bailed him out, time and again,
always swearing that this time was the last, and
always yielding to Delia's entreaties for 'just
one more'.

But just now the atmosphere was genial.
Paulie, on his best behaviour, had recognised
Selena.

'I've seen you riding in the rodeo at—' he
rattled off a list of names. 'Seen you win, too.'

Selena relaxed, managing a smile.

'I don't win much,' she admitted. 'But
enough to keep going.'

'You're a star,' Paulie said, taking her hand
and pumping it up and down between his two.
'It surely is an honour to meet you.'

If Selena felt the same she disguised it suc-
cessfully. There was something about Paulie
that laid a disagreeable sheen even over his
attempts to flatter. She thanked him and with-

drew her hand, fighting the temptation to rub it on her jeans. Paulie had a clammy palm.

'Your room is ready now,' Delia said kindly. 'The girls will show you upstairs.'

Carrie and Billie immediately took charge of Selena, drawing her up the huge staircase before she had time to protest. Paulie followed, impossible to shake off, and by the time they reached the best guest bedroom he'd contrived to get in front and throw open the door.

'Only the best for our famous guest,' he carolled facetiously.

Since Selena wasn't famous, and knew it, this only made her look at him askance. Already she could see a neon sign over Paulie's head, reading 'Trouble'. She was glad when Carrie eased her brother out of the room.

She looked around her, made even more uneasy by the magnificence. The large room had been decorated in pink, mauve and white, Delia's favourite colours. The carpet was a delicate pink that made Selena check her boots for mud. The curtains were pink and mauve brocade and the huge four-poster bed was hung with fine white net curtains. It could have slept four, she thought, testing the mattress gingerly. It was so soft and springy that she took a step back. How did anyone sleep on that without bouncing off?

She took a tour of the room, wondering if they'd put her in the wrong place. Perhaps the Queen of England would step out of the wardrobe and say this was really her room.

The bathroom was equally alarming, being frilly and feminine, with a tub shaped like a huge seashell. If there was one thing Selena knew she wasn't, it was frilly and feminine. She would have preferred a shower, but the cap wasn't quite big enough to protect the dressing on her forehead, so she ran a bath.

When it was just right she climbed in gingerly, relishing the comfort of sinking into the hot water and feeling it soothe her bruises. She sorted her way through the profusion of soaps until she found the least heavily perfumed and began to lather herself with it. Gradually the turmoil of the day slipped away from her. Maybe there was something to be said for soft living after all. Not much, but something.

A row of glass jars stood along a shelf just above the bath, each filled with crystals of a different colour. Curious, she took one down, unscrewed the top and gagged at the aroma, which was even more overpowering than the soap. Gasping, she hastened to replace the top, but her fingers were too slippery to grip properly and the jar slipped straight through them, down into the water and crashed against the bath with an ominous splintering sound. The shock, coming on top of everything else, surprised a yell from her.

Leo, settling into his own room across the hall, was undressing for a shower and had just stripped off his shirt when he heard the yell and paused. Stepping out into the corridor, he stopped again, listening. Silence. Then, from behind Selena's door came a despairing voice.

'*Oh no! What am I going to do?*'

He knocked on her door. 'Hello? Are you all right?'

Her voice reached him faintly. 'Not really.'

He pushed open the door, but could see nobody inside.

'Hello?'

'In here.' Now he could tell that she was in the bathroom, and he approached the open door gingerly, trying not to gasp from the

sweet, powerful aroma that surged out and surrounded his head like a cloud.

'Is it all right for me to come in?' he asked.

'I'm stuck here forever if you don't.'

Moving cautiously he looked around the
door to the great pink shell. Selena was in the
middle of it, her arms crossed over her chest,
glaring at him with frantic eyes.

'I smashed a jar of crystals,' she said desperately.

He looked around. 'Where?'

'In the bath. There's broken glass everywhere under the water, but I can't see where
it is. I daren't move.'

'OK, don't panic.' He found a white towel
and handed it to her, averting his eyes as she
reached for it.

When she'd covered her top she said, 'You
can look. I'm decent—ish.'

'Can you reach the plug?'

'Not without stretching.'

'Then I'll do it. Don't move. Just tell me
where it is.'

'Between my feet.'

Gingerly he slid his fingers down the inner
surface of the bath, trying to find the plug

without touching her, an almost impossible task. At last he found it and managed to ease it open so that the bath could start draining.

'When the water's gone right down I can start to remove the glass,' he said.

At last it came into view, ugly, sharp pieces, dangerously close to her body. He began to pick them out one by one. It was a long process because the jar had smashed into dozens of fragments, and the movement of the water meant that as he cleared one place of tiny, threatening shards, it filled up again with others. Gradually the level dropped, and more of her came into view, which gave him another problem…

'I'm trying not to look, but I really do need to see what I'm doing,' he said desperately.

'Do what you have to,' she agreed.

He took a deep breath. The towel could only cover so much of her, and the water was vanishing fast.

'I've shifted all I can,' Leo said at last. 'You've got to get out by only moving upward, not sideways.'

'But how can I? I shall have to shift around to get my balance, and hold onto something.'

'You hold onto me.' He leaned down. 'Put your arms around my neck.'

She did so, and the towel immediately slithered away.

'Forget it,' Leo said. 'I'm trying to be a gentleman, but would you rather be safe or modest?'

'Safe,' she said at once. 'Let's go.'

She gripped her hands behind his neck and felt his hands on her waist. They were big hands, and they almost encompassed her tiny span. Slowly he straightened up, drawing her with him. She was pressed right against him now, trying not to be too conscious of her bare breasts against his chest, and the way the light covering of hair tickled her.

A bit more, a bit more. Inch by inch they were managing it. The last of the water vanished, revealing a very nasty piece of glass that he'd missed. Selena looked down, horrified, then tried to kick it away.

It was a fatal error. The next moment her foot had slithered from under her and she was falling. But Leo tightened one arm about her, and with the other he reached down, grabbed her behind, and stepped away so fast that he was caught off balance. He staggered back out of the bathroom and for several wild steps he fought to stay upright. But it was no good. The next moment he was on his back on the plush pink carpet, with Selena sprawled naked on top of him.

'Oh God!' she shivered, clinging onto him and forgetting about modesty, about everything except that wicked looking spike.

He held on to her, breathing hard, trying to regain his equilibrium which was whirling away into space, among the stars and planets, wild, glorious, dizzying. The feel of her on top of him was both scary and wonderful, and he knew he had to put a stop to it, fast.

Then his blood froze at an ominous sound.

A female giggle. Two female giggles. Right outside the door.

'Selena,' came Carrie's voice. 'Can we come in?'

'*No!*' Selena's voice rose to a yelp and she jumped up. She just made it to the door in time, reaching out to turn the key.

There wasn't one. The door didn't lock.

Disaster!

'Don't come in, I'm not decent,' she called, putting her back against the door and pushing. 'I'll be down in a minute. Please tell your mom thank you, for me.'

To their relief the voices faded away.

Leo pulled himself together, wondering how much more he could stand. If holding her against him on the floor hadn't destroyed his nervous system, watching her streak across the room like a gazelle had nearly finished him off.

But it had been useful in ascertaining one thing.

His rescue had been successful. There wasn't a scratch on her anywhere.

She dashed into the bathroom and returned in a towelling robe, which mercifully enveloped her.

'Thanks,' she said. 'You saved me from something very nasty.'

He'd gotten to his feet. 'I'd better go before both our reputations are ruined.'

'What am I going to say to Mrs Hanworth?'

'Leave that to me. I don't think you should go downstairs at all. Go to bed. That's an order.'

He checked the corridor and was relieved to find it empty. But no sooner had he stepped out than Carrie and Billie appeared, almost as though they'd been hiding around the corner.

'Hi Leo! Everything OK?'

'Not quite,' he said, horribly conscious that he was only half dressed, and trying not to go red. 'Selena dropped one of the glass jars into the bath, while she was in it, and it smashed.'

'Poor Selena! Is she still trapped in there?'

'No, I got her out, and she's safe,' he said, wishing the earth would swallow him up. 'I promised her I'd tell your mom about the jar. I'll do that—er—just as soon as I've put on a shirt.'

He got into his room as fast as he could, trying not to hear two teenage girls snickering significantly. It was a sound calculated to freeze a man's blood.

Delia reacted just as Leo had known she would, with sympathy and kindness.

'What's a jar?' she said. 'I'll go and make sure she's all right.'

She was back in a few minutes, sweeping into the kitchen to order food to be taken upstairs to Selena. She seemed to have spoken to her daughters in the meantime, for her attitude to Leo had developed a tinge of roguishness.

'I gather you played knight in shining armour. And who could blame you? She's a very nice-looking girl.'

'Delia, I swear I never met her before today.'

Fatal mistake. Delia smiled knowingly. 'You Italians are so dashing and romantic, never missing a chance with the ladies.'

'What are those wonderful smells coming from the kitchen?' he asked desperately, 'because you are looking at a starving man.'

Mercifully food was allowed to drive out all other topics of conversation, and the only other person who raised the matter was Paulie, who nudged Leo aside and said much the same as his mother, except that he made it sound vulgar and offensive. When Leo had smilingly explained to Paulie all the unpleasant things he would do to his person if he ever mentioned it again, the matter was allowed to drop.

While he dressed for the barbecue Leo tried to get his own reactions in perspective. Despite her prickly defensiveness, for which he reckoned nobody could blame her, Selena was oddly appealing. But there wasn't, at first glance, anything special about her. Even holding her naked body shouldn't have been a big deal, since she lacked the buxomness he preferred in women.

Yet, mysteriously, something about her had got to him. He still couldn't figure out what, but the sight of Paulie smacking his fat lips over what he thought had gone on in her room had filled him with rage. Leo, the most amiable of men, had only been restrained from violence by recalling that this was his hostess's son.

Guests were starting to arrive, heading for the field where the big party was taking place, the same field where last night's big party had taken place, and where there would be another one just as soon as someone could think of an excuse. Leo watched it from his window, grinning, anticipating the evening.

'Ready for a great time?' Barton hollered as Leo came down the stairs.

'I'm always ready for that,' Leo said, truthfully. 'But can we call in at the stables first?'

'Sure, if you want. But Leo, you don't have to worry. She's going to be all right.'

'Elliot's a he.'

'It wasn't Elliot I was meaning,' Barton said, seeming to speak to nobody in particular.

The anti-inflammatory drug was evidently taking effect, and Elliot seemed contented. The way to the barbecue field led past Barton's garage, and through the open door Leo could see Selena's van, and the remains of the horse trailer.

'That's had its day,' Barton mused. 'The wonder is, how it lasted so long.'

Leo climbed into the van. What he saw there made him grow very still.

He thought of himself as a man who could cope with tough living, but the inside of her home shocked him. Everything was the barest and meanest possible. There was a couch just long enough for her to sleep, a tiny stove, a minute washing area. The best that could be said for the place was that it was spotlessly clean.

His own experiences of living rough, he realised, had been those of a rich man, playing with a kind of toy. However harsh the conditions, he could always return to a comfortable life when he got bored with playing. But for her there was no escape. This was her reality.

What could have made her choose the life of a wanderer, which seemed to offer her so little?

One thing was becoming horribly clear. The accident had robbed her of almost everything she had.

After that he had no chance to think gloomy thoughts. Texas hospitality opened its arms to him, and he rushed into them, enjoying every moment, and telling himself he'd have time to be exhausted later. What with plentiful food and drink, music and pretty girls to dance with, several hours slipped happily away.

When he could pause for breath he wondered how Selena was fixed? Had she eaten the supper Delia sent up, and was she hungry again?

He piled a plate high with steak and potatoes, tucked some cans of beer under his arm and headed for the house. But some instinct made him check the stables—just in case. As he'd half expected, Selena was there, leaning on the door of Elliot's stall, just watching him contentedly.

'How is he?' Leo asked, looking in.

She jumped up. 'He's better. He's calmed down a lot.'

She was better too, he could see that. Her cheeks had colour and her eyes were bright. He raised the plate to show her and she eyed the steak hungrily.

'That for me?'

'Well, it sure as hell isn't for Elliot. Come on out.'

He found a solid bale of hay and they sat down together. He handed her a beer and she tipped her head back to take most of it in one go.

'Oh, that was good!' she sighed.

'Well, there's plenty more out there,' he said, indicating the door with his head. 'In fact there's plenty of steaks too. Why not come out and join the party?'

'Thanks, but I won't.'

'Still not feeling up to partying?'

'No, I'm better. I slept well. It's just—all those people, looking at me and thinking my voice isn't right, and—everything isn't right.'

'Who says you're not right?'

'I do. This house—everything—it gives me the heebie-jeebies.'

'You've never been in a house like that before?'

'Oh, sure, plenty of times. Just not through the front door. I've worked in places like this, mopping floors, cleaning up in the kitchen, anything that was going. Mind you, I preferred a job in the stable.'

'When was this? You talk like you were ancient, but you can't be more than forty.'

'More than—?' She saw the wicked gleam in his eyes, and laughed. 'I'd thump you if you weren't sitting between me and the beer.'

'That's what I like,' he said, handing her another can. 'A woman with a sense of priorities. So, not forty then?'

'I'm twenty-six.'

'And when was all this ancient history?'

'I've been looking after myself since I was fourteen.'

'Shouldn't you have been at school?'

Another shrug. 'I suppose.'

'What happened to your parents?'

After a few moment's silence she said, 'I was raised in a home, several actually.'

'You mean you're an orphan?'

'Probably not. Nobody knew who my father was. Not sure even my mom knew that. All I really knew about her was that she was just a kid herself when she had me, couldn't cope, put me in a home. I expect she meant to come back for me, but things got too much for her.' Selena took another swig.

'And what then?' Leo asked, in the grip of an appalled fascination.

'Foster homes.'

'Homes? Plural?'

'The first one was OK. That's where I found out about horses. After that I knew whatever I did it had to be with horses. But the old man died and the stock got sold off and I was sent somewhere else. That was bad. The food was rotten and I was cheap labour, kept off from school because they were too mean to pay an extra hand. I told them where they could stick it and they sent me packing. Said I was "out of control". Which was true. In a pig's ear I was going to let them control me.'

'But aren't there laws to protect kids in this situation?'

She looked at him as if he was crazy.

'Of course there are laws,' she said patiently. 'And inspectors to see that the laws are followed.'

'So?'

'So bad things happen anyway. Some of the inspectors are decent people, but they get swamped. There's just too much to do. And some of them just see what they want to see because that way they finish work early.'

She spoke lightly, without bitterness, like someone describing life on another planet. Leo was aghast. His own existence in Italy, a country where family ties were still stronger than almost anywhere else, seemed like paradise in comparison.

'What happened after that?' he asked, in a daze.

She shrugged again and he realised how eloquent her shrugs were, each one seeming to contain a whole speech.

'A new foster home, no different. I ran away, got caught and sent back to the institution, and after a while there was another foster home. That lasted three weeks.'

'What then?' he asked, for she'd fallen silent again.

'This time I made sure they didn't catch me. I was fourteen and could pass for sixteen. I don't suppose they looked for me long. You know, this steak is really good.'

He accepted her change of subject without protest. Why should she want to discuss her life if it had been like that?

CHAPTER THREE

Now that her fear for Elliot had been eased Selena was growing more relaxed, exuding an air of taking life as it came that Leo guessed was more normal with her.

'Have you and Elliot been together long?' he asked.

'Five years. I got some work doing odd jobs about the rodeos, and bought him cheap from a guy who owed me money. He reckoned Elliot's career was over, but I thought he still had good things in him if he was treated right. And I do treat him right.'

'I guess he appreciates that,' Leo said as she rose and went to fondle Elliot's nose. The horse pressed forward to her.

He rose too and began to stroll along the stalls, looking in at the animals, who gazed back, peaceful, beautiful, almost seeming to glow in the dim light.

'You know about horses,' Selena asked, joining him. 'I could tell.'

'I breed a few, back home.'

'Where's home?'

'Italy.'

'Then you really are a foreigner.'

He grinned. 'Couldn't you tell by my "funny accent"?'

She gave a sudden blazing grin. 'It's not as funny as some I've heard.'

It was as though the sun had come up with her smile. Wanting to make her laugh, Leo went into a clowning version of Italian. Seizing her hand he kissed the back and crooned theatrically,

'*Bella signorina*, letta me tell you abouta my country. In Eeetaly we know 'ow to appreciate a beautiful lai-ee-dy.'

She stared, more flabbergasted than impressed.

'You *talk* like that in Italy?'

'No, of course not,' he said, reverting to his normal voice. 'But when we're abroad it's how we're expected to talk.'

'Only by folk who need their heads examined.'

'Well, I meet a lot of them. Most people's ideas about Italians come straight out of cliché. We're not all bottom pinchers.'

'No, you just wink at women on the highway.'

'Who does?'

'You do. Did. When Mr Hanworth's car passed me, I saw you looking at me, and you winked.'

'Only because you winked first.'

'I did not,' she said, up in arms.

'You did.'

'I did not.'

'I saw you.'

'It was a trick of the light. I do not wink at strange men.'

'And I don't wink at strange women—unless they wink at me first.'

Suddenly she began to laugh, just as he'd wanted her to, and the sun came out again. He took her hand and led her back to the bale where they'd been sitting, and they clinked beer cans.

'Tell me about your home,' she said. 'Where in Italy?'

'Tuscany, the northern part, near the coast. I have a farm, breed some horses, grow some grapes. Ride in the rodeo.'

'Rodeo? In Italy? You're kidding me.'

'No way! We have a little town called Grosseto, which has a rodeo every year, complete with a parade through the town. There's a building there with walls covered with photos of the local "cowboys". Until I was six I thought all cowboys were Italian. When my cousin Marco told me they came from the States I called him a liar. We had to be separated by our parents.'

He paused, for she was choking with laughter.

'In the end,' he said, 'I had to come and see the real thing.'

'Got any family, apart from your cousin?'

'Some. Not a wife. I live alone except for Gina.'

'She's a live-in girlfriend?'

'No, she's over fifty. She cooks and cleans and makes dire predictions about how I'll never find a wife because no younger woman will put up with that draughty building.'

'Are the draughts really bad?'

'They are in winter. Thick stone walls and flagstones to walk on.'

'Sounds really primitive.'

'I guess it is. It was built eight hundred years ago and as soon as I finish one repair it seems I have to start another. But in summer it's beautiful. That's when you appreciate the stone keeping you cool. And when you go out in the early morning and look down the valley, there's a soft light that you see at no other time. But you have to be there at exactly the right moment, because it only lasts a few minutes. Then the light changes, becomes harsher, and if you want to see the magic again you have to go back next morning.'

He stopped, slightly surprised at himself for using so many words, and for the almost poetic strain of feeling that had come through them. He realised that she was looking at him with gentle interest.

'Tell me more,' she said. 'I like listening to people talk about what they love.'

'Yes, I suppose I do love it,' he said thoughtfully. 'I love the whole life, even though it's demanding, and sometimes rough and uncomfortable. At harvest you get up at dawn and go to bed when you're in a state of collapse, but I wouldn't have it any other way.'

'You got brothers, sisters?'

'I've got a younger brother—' Leo grinned '—although technically Guido is the elder. In fact, legally I barely exist because it turned out my parents weren't married, only nobody knew at the time.'

She made a quick, alert movement. 'You mean you're a bastard too?'

'Yes, I guess I am.'

'Do you care?'

'Not in the slightest.'

'Me neither,' she said contentedly. 'It sort of leaves you free. You can go where you want and do what you want, be who you want. Do you find it's like that?'

Receiving no answer she turned to look at Leo and found him leaned right back, his eyes closed, his body stretched out in an attitude of abandon. Jet lag wouldn't be fought off any longer.

Selena reached out to nudge him awake, but stopped with her hand an inch away, and watched him. The day's turbulent events had left her no chance to consider him at leisure.

He'd been the rescuer who'd caught up with Elliot, when she herself might not have done so in time, and whose gentle hands and voice had calmed the animal. If her beloved Elliot accepted him then she must too.

In the bathroom he'd saved her from nasty injury. Beyond that she hadn't allowed herself to think. But she could think about it now, how it had felt to be held tightly against him, the soft scratching of the hairs on his chest against her bare breasts. She could remember, too, the bold way he'd grasped her behind with his big hand, hauling her to safety and removing his hand at once.

A gentleman, she thought. Even at that moment.

Everything about him pleased her, starting with the broad sweep of his forehead, half hidden now by a lock of hair that had fallen over it, and the heavy brows, and the dark-brown eyes beneath them. She liked the straight nose and the slightly heavy curved mouth that could smile in a way that hinted at delight to come for a woman with a brave spirit.

She wondered just how brave her own spirit was. In the ring she would take any risk, dare any fall, chance any unfamiliar horse, and laugh. But folk were different, harder to understand than horses. They were awkward and they could hurt you more than any tumble.

And yet she wanted to see Leo's smile again, and follow the tempting hints to their conclusion.

She liked his foreignness, his faint Italian accent, his way of pronouncing certain words in a way that was strange to her, but delightful. She wanted to know him better, to discover more about the big, generously proportioned body, and to realise the promise implicit in those broad shoulders and lean, hard torso. As if drawn by a magnet her eyes fell on his hands, and memories sprang alive in her flesh. Those long fingers, touching her nakedness as he lifted her out of the bath. They seemed to be touching her now, this minute. She could feel them....

Hell, who did she think she was kidding? Everyone knew that Italians liked curvy females, with hour-glass figures.

And I don't have any in-and-out, she reminded herself sorrowfully. Just 'in.' And he's seen me now, so there's no way to fool him.

Life was very hard!

Elliot whinnied softly, and the sound was enough to awaken Leo. He opened his eyes while her face was still close to his, and smiled.

'I've died and gone to heaven,' he said. 'And you're an angel.'

'I don't think they'll be sending me to heaven. Not unless someone's changed the rules.'

They both laughed, and she went to Elliot, who had whinnied again.

'He's just jealous because you're giving me so much attention,' Leo said.

'He's got nothing to be jealous about, and he knows it,' Selena said. 'He's my family.'

'Where do you live?'

'Wherever Elliot and I happen to be.'

'But you must have some sort of home base, where you stay when you're not travelling?'

'Nope.'

'You mean, you're travelling all the time?'

'Yup.'

'With no home to go to?' he asked, aghast.

'I've got a place where I'm registered for paying taxes. But I don't live there. I live with

Elliot. He's my home as well as my family. And he always will be.'

'It can't be ''always'',' he pointed out. 'I don't know how old he is, but—'

'He's not old,' Selena said quickly. 'He looks older than he is because he's a bit battered, but that's all.'

'Yes, I'm sure,' Leo said gently. 'But just how old is he?'

She sighed. 'I'm not sure. But he's not finished yet.' She laid her cheek against Elliot's nose. 'They don't know you like I do,' she whispered, and turned her head away so that he couldn't see the anguish that swamped her.

But he did see it, and his heart ached for her. That raw-boned animal, past his best, was all she had in the world to love.

Suddenly her strength seemed to drain away. Leo quickly took hold of her.

'That's it, you're going to bed. Don't argue because I won't take no for an answer.'

He kept his arm firmly fixed about her waist in case she had any other ideas, but she was too weary to argue, and let him lead her away to the house and up the stairs to her room.

'Goodnight,' he said at her door. 'Sleep well.'

'Leo, you don't understand,' she confided in a low voice. 'I can't sleep in that bed. It's too soft. Every time I move it bounces.'

His lips twitched. 'They're supposed to. Still, I know what you mean. If it's not what you're used to it can be worse than stones. You'll just have to try to put up with all this comfort. You'll get used to it.'

'Not me,' she said with conviction, and slipped into her room.

He stood looking at the closed door, a prey to unfamiliar feelings that confused him. He wanted to follow her into her bedroom, not to have his evil way, but to ask her to lay her problems on him, and promise to make everything right for her.

Having his evil way could come later. When he'd earned the right.

It was almost dawn when the last guest drove away, waving an arm out of the window and yodelling, 'See ya!' Bleary eyed and cheerful, the household drifted off to bed.

Leo sat down on his bed with a feeling of pleasant vagueness. The evening had contained much bourbon and rye, especially the last part, after he'd said goodnight to Selena and returned to the festivities. Now he was at peace with the world.

But he didn't miss the sound of footsteps that stopped outside Selena's bedroom door. A pause, then a soft creak as the door was opened. That was enough to make Leo's tipsy haze pass, and send him out into the corridor in time to catch Paulie halfway through Selena's door.

'Why, isn't this nice?' he said in a voice that made Paulie jump. 'Both of us so concerned about Selena that we couldn't sleep until we knew she was fine.'

Paulie gave him a glassy smile. 'Can't neglect a guest.'

'Paulie, you're an example to us all.'

Leo was moving into the room as he spoke, switching on the light. Then both men stopped, taken aback by the sight of the empty bed.

'That tomfool female has gone back to the stables,' Leo muttered.

'No I haven't,' came from a heap on the floor.

Leo switched on the bedside light and saw the heap separate itself into its various parts, which included a blanket, a pillow, and one tomfool female whose red hair stood up on her head in a shock.

'What is it?' she asked, sitting up. 'Has something happened?'

'No, Paulie and I were concerned for you, so we came to see how you were.'

'That's very kind,' she said, guessing the truth at once. 'I'm fine.'

'She's fine, Paulie. You can go to bed now, and sleep tight.' Leo sat down on the floor beside Selena with the air of a man taking root.

'Er—well, I just—'

'Goodnight, Paulie.' They spoke as one.

Forced to accept defeat, Paulie backed himself out of the door. The last thing they saw was his scowl.

'I could have coped, you know,' Selena said.

'When you're well, I'm sure you could,' Leo said tactfully. 'But let's wait until then.

Underneath Paulie's flabby exterior there's a very ugly customer waiting to get out.'

'I reckoned that. But that's three times in one day you've come galloping to my rescue. I just don't want you to think I'm a wimp.'

'After the day you've had, aren't you entitled to be just a bit of a wimp?'

'Nobody is entitled to be a wimp.'

'Sorry!'

'No, I'm sorry,' she said contritely. 'I didn't mean to be rude. I know you were trying to be kind, but all this rescuing is getting to be a bad habit.'

'I promise not to do it again. Next time I'll abandon you to your fate, I swear.'

'Do that.'

'Are you all right on the floor?'

'I put up with the bed as long as I could,' she complained, 'but it's insane. Every time I turned over I went six feet in the air. This is much better.'

'I'd better leave before I fall asleep.' Suddenly he found himself vague. 'Where am I? Is the party over?'

'Must be.' She smiled, fully understanding. 'Was the whisky very good?'

'Barton's whisky is always good. And I should know. I had plenty of it.'

'Shall I help you back to your room?'

'I think I can make it. Lock your door when I'm gone. I wouldn't put it past Delia's little boy to try again.'

But then he remembered that the door it didn't lock. He sighed. There was only one thing for it.

'What are you doing?' she asked as he returned to the bed and scooped up a blanket and pillow.

'What does it look as if I'm doing?' he said, dropping to the floor and stretching out across the door. 'If he can open this door now he's a better man than I take him for.'

'You promised to leave me to my fate next time,' she reminded him indignantly.

'I know, but you can't trust a word I say.'

Blessed sleep was overtaking him. His last coherent thought was that he'd be made to suffer for this in the morning.

But at least she would be safe.

He awoke feeling better than he had any right to after what he recalled of the barbecue.

Already he could sense the house stirring about him, and reckoned it was safe to leave her.

It was better to be gone before she awoke. He wouldn't have known what to say to her. Inside him he was jeering at himself for going into what he ironically called 'chivalrous mode'.

That was something he'd never done before in his life. The women whose company he sought were cut from the same cloth as himself, and after much the same things. Fun, laughter, uncomplicated pleasure, a good time had by all, and no hearts broken. It had always worked beautifully.

Until now.

Now, suddenly, he found himself acting like a knight in shining armour, and it worried him.

Chivalry or no, he dropped gently down beside her sleeping form, and studied her face. Her colour had improved since last night and he could see that she slept, as he always did himself, dead to the world, like a contented animal.

She'd removed her dressing, so that the cut and bruise on her forehead showed up starkly against her pallor. She had a funny little face, he thought, right now looking as vulnerable as child's, with the caution and worldly wisdom smoothed from it by sleep.

He reflected on the story she'd told him the night before, and guessed that she'd learned too much of the world in one way, and not enough in another.

He had an almost overmastering desire to lean down and kiss her, but the next moment he was glad he hadn't, because she opened her eyes. They were wonderful eyes, large and sea deep, and they made the child vanish.

'Hi,' he said. 'I'm off now. When I've showered I'll go downstairs, trying to look like a man who slept in his own room. Perhaps you should try to look as if you slept in this bed, for Delia's sake.'

'You think she'd be offended?'

'No, I think she'd be afraid the bed wasn't soft enough, and heaven knows what you'd find on it tonight.'

They laughed, and he helped her up. She was wearing a man's shirt that came down almost to her knees.

'How are you feeling this morning?' he asked.

'Great. I just had the most comfortable night of my life.'

'On the floor?'

'This carpet is inches thick. Perfect.'

'Cross your fingers that I don't get seen leaving here.'

'I'll check the corridor for you.'

She looked and gave him the thumbs up. It took just a brief moment to dash back to his own room, and safety. True, he thought he heard the girls giggling again, but that was probably just paranoia.

He showered and dressed in a mood that was unusually thoughtful, for him, because he was uneasily aware that he didn't have a completely clear conscience. Without actually saying anything untrue he'd left Selena with the impression that he was almost as poor as herself. She'd seen him in worn clothing, heard him talk about living rough, and taken on board the fact that he was illegitimate.

But he'd neglected to mention that his uncle was Count Calvani, with a palace in Venice, and his family were millionaires. What he had casually referred to as his farm was a rich-man's estate, and if he helped out with the rough work it was because he preferred it that way.

He hadn't made these things clear because of a deep, instinctive conviction that they would have made her think badly of him.

He remembered her words, just after the accident.

'You're all the same. You rush around in your flash cars as though you owned the road.'

His car back home was a heavy duty, four-wheel drive, suitable for the hills of Tuscany. A working man's car, but a rich working man, who'd bought the best because he never bought anything else. In that he was a true Calvani, and now his sense of self-preservation was telling him that this would be fatal in Selena's eyes.

And why risk a falling out when he would only be here a couple of weeks, and then they would never see each other again?

In the end he did the only thing a sensible man could possibly do.

Pushed it to the back of his mind and hoped for the best.

He spent the day with Barton, riding his friend's acres. Barton reared cattle for money and horses for love; he bred and trained them for the rodeo.

Leo's eye was taken by a chestnut. He was a quarter horse, short, muscular, bred for speed over a quarter mile, the perfect barrel racer.

'Beautiful, isn't he?' Barton said as they looked him over. 'He came from here originally, bought by the wife of a friend of mine. I bought him back when she gave up the rodeo to have kids.'

'Can we take him back with us, and put him in the stable?' Leo asked thoughtfully.

Barton nodded, but as they rode home he mused, 'My friend, you are getting in over your head.'

'C'mon Barton, you know what the insurance guys are going to say. They'll take one look at Elliot and one at the van, and when they've stopped laughing they'll offer her ten cents.'

'And what's it to you? None of it was your fault.'

'She's going to lose everything.'

'Yes, but what's it to you?'

Leo ground his teeth. 'Can we just get home?'

Barton grinned.

They arrived to find a mood of gloom. Selena was sitting on the step of her van, staring at the ground while the two girls tried to comfort her, and Paulie hovered, clucking.

'The vet says Elliot won't be well enough for her to ride next week,' Carrie said. 'If she tries, it could really injure him.'

'Of course I won't do that,' Selena said at once. 'But now I'll have no chance to win anything, and I must owe you so much—'

'Now, now, none of that,' Barton said. 'The insurance—'

'The insurance will just about buy me a wheelbarrow and a donkey,' Selena said with a wry smile. She pointed to her forehead. 'I'm over this now. I can face the truth.'

'We won't know the truth until you've ridden a couple of races,' Barton declared.

'On what?' With a faint attempt at comedy she added, 'I don't have the donkey yet.'

'No, but you can do me a favour.' Barton indicated the quarter horse. 'His name's Jeepers. I've got a buyer interested, and if he wins a barrel race or two I can up the price. So you ride him, show him off, and that'll more than repay me.'

'He's beautiful,' Selena breathed, running her hands lovingly over the animal. 'Not as beautiful as Elliot of course,' she added quickly.

'Of course not,' Leo said gently.

'He's well trained,' Barton told her. He explained the story of the previous owner and Selena was scandalised.

'She gave up the rodeo to stay in one place and have babies?'

'Some women are funny like that,' Leo observed, grinning.

Selena's look showed him what she thought of such an idea. 'Can I put my saddle on him now?'

'Good idea.'

While Selena got to work Leo drew Barton aside.

'So tell me about this mysterious buyer,' he said.

Barton looked him full in the eye.

'You know who's gonna buy that horse, as well as I do,' he said.

*   *   *

The whole family turned out to watch Selena try out Jeepers in Barton's testing ring. The three barrels were set up in a triangle, with one side of ninety feet, and the other two sides one hundred and five feet each. Selena and Jeepers came flying across the starting line, into the triangle, turned sharply right around the first barrel, back into the triangle, around the second barrel, turned left and headed up the centre for the last barrel.

Each turn was a tight forty-five degrees, testing a horse's balance and agility as well as speed. Jeepers was swift yet steady as a rock, and Selena controlled him with light, strong hands. Even Leo, no expert in barrel racing, could see that they were a match made in heaven.

After the final turn they headed back down the centre of the triangle, and out, to the cheers of the family and the hands.

'Eighteen seconds,' Barton called.

Selena's eyes were shining. 'We took it slow the first time. Wait till we get going. It'll be fourteen in no time.'

She let out a joyous *'Yahoooo!'* up to the sky and everyone joined her.

Leo, watching her face, thought he'd never seen any human being look so totally happy.

CHAPTER FOUR

SELENA had said there was no excuse for being a wimp, and over the next few days she lived up to her belief. She brushed off her injury with the airiness of someone who'd had worse and ignored it, and she rode hell-for-leather on Jeepers until she'd gotten his time down to fourteen seconds, just as she'd vowed.

Barton insisted that she stay at the Four-Ten until after the rodeo. This made sense as Elliot's recovery was slow, and she had no money to go anywhere else, but privately he gave Leo a wink, proving there was more to his offer than kindness.

'It's all in your head,' Leo growled when they were alone. 'Sure I like the girl, sure I want to help her. Dammit, nobody ever did until us! But that doesn't mean—'

'Of course not,' Barton said, and went on his way whistling.

Leo had a horrible suspicion that the events of the first night had somehow become known throughout the house, which meant that Billie and Carrie's giggling meant something after all. Paulie clearly thought so, because his manner towards Leo became cool.

Leo dropped in at the stables each evening, knowing he'd find Selena there, saying goodnight to Elliot. She always did this at length, and Leo was privately convinced that she was trying to make sure that he knew he still came first with her, despite Jeepers. Sometimes she stayed all night.

But tonight something was different. Instead of her softly murmuring voice he could hear the sounds of a scuffle as he pushed open the stable door. Somewhere deep in the shadows a fight was going on.

After a moment he saw the two combatants. There was Selena, fending off advances from Paulie, who wouldn't take no for an answer.

'C'mon, stop fooling. I've seen the looks you've been giving me. I know when a woman wants it.'

He made a lunge. Leo swore under his breath and gathered himself to spring on Paulie, a knight coming to the rescue of a damsel in distress.

But this damsel needed no such help. There was a yell from Paulie, who went reeling back, clutching his nose, while Selena blew on her knuckles.

'Nice,' Leo mused. 'I'll make a note not to get on your wrong side. Not that I planned to anyway, but now I've had my warning.'

'He asked for it,' Selena said, still blowing.

'Not a doubt.'

Abruptly her manner changed. 'But I shouldn't have done it,' she said. 'Oh, lord, I wish I hadn't.'

'What for?' Leo demanded. 'Why stop when you're having fun? And I should think socking him must have been great fun. I'm green with envy.'

'But they'll throw me out,' she said frantically. 'And Elliot's not ready to go. Do you think if I apologised—?'

He stared at her. Talk of an apology was the last thing he'd expected from her.

'Apologise? You?'

'I can't move Elliot yet. Let me talk to that creature.'

'No, let me,' he said, taking firm hold of her and keeping her where she was.

He strolled over to where Paulie had just staggered upright, glaring over a hand that was clutched to his nose.

'How y'doing, Paulie?' Leo asked affably.

Paulie carefully lowered his hand, revealing a red, enlarged nose and streaming eyes.

'Did you see what she did?' he snarled.

'Yes, and I saw what you did. I'd say you'd gotten off lightly.'

'That bitch—'

'Well, you can always have your revenge,' Leo observed, studying the injured proboscis with interest. 'Just go back and tell Mommy that you got slugged in the kisser by a woman. I'll be your witness. In fact I'll make sure the story's known all over Texas. It'll probably get into the newspapers. Of course they'll want a picture of you looking just as you do now.'

There was a deadly silence while Paulie digested the implications of this. His piggy eyes, full of spite, went from one to the other.

'What do you take me for?' he snapped at last.

'If I told you what I took you for we'd be here all night,' Leo said.

Paulie wisely decided to overlook this.

'She's a guest here. Naturally I shall—' he almost choked over the last words '—say nothing.'

'I felt sure you'd see it that way. A gentleman to the end. And if anyone asks how you got that shiner you can say you tripped on a pitchfork. Or tell them I did it, I don't mind.'

'But I do,' Selena protested. 'In a pig's ear you're getting the credit. If I can't take it myself, he'll have to say it was a pitchfork.'

Leo grinned, delighted with her. 'Atta girl,' he said softly.

'You're crazy, the pair of you,' Paulie howled.

Giving them a wide berth he sidled his way out of the stable, breaking into a run as soon as he was out of the door.

'Thank you,' Selena said fervently. 'That was terrific.'

'Glad to be of some help. I should have knocked him down for you, but you didn't seem to need me.'

'Oh, I can do that bit for myself,' she said blithely. 'It's the words that confuse me. You knew just what to say to keep him quiet. I never know what to say. The more I try, the more it comes out wrong.'

'Better with your fists, huh?'

'I've had plenty of practise.'

He appeared to consider the matter seriously. 'I'd have guessed you to be more of a knee in the groin girl, myself.'

She regarded him steadily. 'I use whatever weapons are needed.'

'I suppose this kind of thing happens to you a lot?'

'Some guys think a woman travelling alone is fair game. I just show them that they're wrong.'

She spoke lightly, with another of her eloquent shrugs. In some mysterious way that shrug hurt him, with its implied acceptance of all the risks. He thought of her lonely life, always on the move, with only a horse to love. Yet he knew that if she guessed that he was concerned for her she would be incredulous. She would probably accuse him of being sentimental.

Then it occurred to him that she didn't even realise that she was lonely. She'd known noth-

ing else. And that hurt him more than anything.

Selena watched him, trying to read his
thoughts. It irked her not to be able to. Men
were usually so easy to read.

She shook her hand, flexing the fingers, and
he took it between his, massaging it between
his strong, warm palms. She stood there, feeling peace and contentment flood her, almost
for the first time in her life. It was a blissful
feeling.

'Are you all right?' he asked.

'Everything's fine,' she assured him.

'Until the next time.'

'Hey, you didn't save me. I saved myself,'
she said at once.

'Will you stop being so prickly? Am I the
enemy?'

She shook her head, softened, smiling at
him. Moved by an impulse too strong for him,
Leo enfolded her in his arms, where she almost
vanished. He cradled her carefully, longing to
hold her there for ever, desperate to kiss her,
but knowing that he mustn't do it while she
was so vulnerable.

Selena could hear his heart beating and the sound comforted her. It would have been so easy to lean on this big, generous man, and let him shoulder her problems.

If she had been that kind of female. Which she wasn't. If she knew anything about herself, she knew that.

She looked up and saw the sudden trouble in his face.

'What is it?' she whispered.

He leaned down so that his forehead rested on hers. From here, a kiss was only an inch away, and she waited, wanting it to happen.

'Nothing,' he said. 'I was just wishing—no, nothing's the matter.'

'Leo—' she reached up, but he raised his head quickly.

'You've got to stop sleeping out here,' he said, releasing her and stepping back. 'It's too easy for him to get at you.'

She took a moment to still the pang of disappointment at his rejection.

'He can do that in the house,' she said. 'Unless you sleep across my door again.'

'No, that's not a good idea,' he said desperately. He'd shared her room once without trying to get into her bed, but he knew he couldn't trust himself to do it again.

'Let's go,' he said, leading the way out, keeping his distance from her.

All the way across the yard she lectured herself silently about staying level-headed. So she didn't attract him? Well, she'd known that! And the pain in her heart could have been saved if she hadn't indulged in silly fantasies.

She kept this up until they reached the house and she could assume a sensible manner, and listen to Delia telling how poor Paulie had stepped on a pitchfork and bruised his nose.

Leo made a point of getting Selena alone next morning.

'Let's ride,' he said. 'I want to try out one of Barton's horses over a distance.'

He had an ulterior motive, since he'd connived with Barton to get her away while the insurance assessors came to look things over. He had a fair idea what would happen then, and he needed time to sort out his thoughts.

He'd seen her racing around barrels and been impressed. Now he could watch her at ease, riding for the pleasure of it, and thought how natural and elegant she looked. Even on an unfamiliar horse she rode as though they were one. He thought of a fiery mare of his own back home, and wished he could introduce them.

They raced. He was riding the more powerful animal but he only just beat her. She had the trick of getting the best out of her horse, and Jeepers was at ease with her.

They found a shaded stream and stretched out under the trees with the beer and hot dogs they'd brought with them. Selena took a deep breath and leaned back, thinking how good it felt to be here like this, with the sun, the sparkling water, the invigorated feeling of having ridden for miles.

Get real, she told herself. What you really mean is, to be here with him. You've got windmills in your head. He's not for you. Be strong. You can cope as long as he doesn't talk in that gentle voice that knocks you sideways.

Forewarned should have been forearmed, but she still felt shaken when he asked quietly, 'Are you all right now?'

She meant to pass it off lightly with some remark about how many people were looking after her these days, but his eyes were kind and warm, and suddenly she couldn't joke.

'Yes, I'm feeling really good,' she said. 'It's funny, all the things I ought to be worrying about—I can't make myself think of them. They're still there, but—sort of vague, and in the background.'

'Well, you can't do anything about them at this moment,' he said, 'so why not let yourself float? You may cope better for it.'

'I know but—' she gave an awkward little laugh '—it's not like me. Normally I worry at things like a dog with a bone. Does no good, but I still do it.'

He nodded. 'Worrying's a waste of time.'

'You're not a worrying sort of person, are you?'

He grinned and shook his head ruefully. 'If it happens, it happens. If it doesn't happen, maybe that was for the best.'

'I envy you. Everything matters so much to me. It's like—' She fell silent, wondering at herself. Analysing also wasn't like her. Her thoughts and feelings were her own private property, and she guarded them behind barriers. But something about Leo drew her out from behind those barriers. Into the open. Into places she'd never ventured before. That's why he was a dangerous man, for all his quiet ways.

'Like what?' he asked, watching her with a little smile.

'Nothing.' She was retreating fast.

But he cut off her retreat, taking her hand gently in his, silently telling her she was safe with him.

'Tell me,' he said.

'No, I—I've forgotten what I was going to say.' She laughed awkwardly.

He didn't reply in words, but his raised eyebrows called her a coward.

Take the chance. Trust him.

'It's like all my life I was walking on a tightrope over a chasm,' she blurted out. 'I keep thinking I'll reach the other side but—' She waved her hands. Words came hard to her.

'What's waiting on the other side?' Leo asked, still holding her hand in his.

She met his eyes, shaking her head. 'I'm not sure there is one. Or if there is, I'll never find it.'

'You're wrong about that Selena. There's always another side, but you have to know what you want to find there. You just haven't decided yet. When you've made up your mind, you'll see the far ledge. And you'll get there.'

'Unless I fall off first. I keep feeling myself get wobbly.'

'I can't imagine you getting wobbly.'

'That's because I shout a lot, to hide it. Sometimes, the louder I yell, the more I'm like jelly inside.'

'I don't believe it. You're too gutsy.'

'Thanks but you don't know me.'

'Funny, but I feel as though I do. When we met up on that highway and you bawled me out, it felt like you'd been bawling me out all my life.'

She gave a shaky laugh. 'Yes, I'm good at bawling people out.'

'My back's broad.' He released her hand and leaned back against a tree, looking deeply content, like a man who already had everything life had to offer.

'Leo, doesn't anything faze you?'

'Bad harvests. Bad weather. Big cities. Meanness, dishonesty, unkindness.'

She nodded vigorously. 'Oh, yes.'

He asked suddenly, 'What do you want to do with your life, Selena?'

'I'm doing it.'

'But in the end?'

'You tell me when the end's going to come,' she parried, 'and I'll tell you what I'll be doing.'

'I meant you can't do this forever. One day it'll be too much for you and you'll have to settle down.'

She made a face. 'You mean pipe and slippers?'

He laughed. 'Well, not the pipe if you don't want to.'

'Domesticity. Home and hearth. No thanks! Not me! Four walls make me crazy. Staying in one place makes me even crazier.'

'And the loneliness?'

She gave an incredulous laugh. 'I'm not lonely. I'm free. No, no, don't say it.'

'Don't say what?'

'Something about loneliness and freedom being the same thing. Where does one shade into the other? Will I know the difference before it's too late? Et cetera, et cetera, et cetera.'

'You've heard that line before, huh?'

'A dozen times. It's such a cliché.'

'Well, most clichés are true. That's how they become clichés.'

'But I'm talking about freedom. Nobody telling me what to do. Nobody expects anything of me, except Elliot, and I love him so that's OK.'

'But you might get to love a person,' Leo suggested cautiously, 'maybe almost as much as you love Elliot.'

'Nah, people are tricky. You've got to watch your back all the time. Elliot's better. He keeps it simple.'

'I think you're teasing a rise out of me.' Leo was watching her carefully, like a man trying to decide which way a cat would jump.

'No way. Give me a horse any day. Take the other night in the stable, did you see Elliot trying to paw me about, breathing whisky fumes all over me? Did you hear him neighing, ''Go on Selena, you know you want it really.''?'

'Yes, I heard Paulie's line in charm,' Leo said in disgust. 'You should have socked him with both fists.'

'No need. He got the message after one. I don't like unnecessary violence. It's wasteful and it hurts your hands.' She added mischievously, 'Never use two fists where one will do. I learned that early.'

'I guess you've learned a lot of things most women never need to.'

She nodded.

'You still haven't answered my question,' Leo said. 'What will you do when you have to give up rodeo?'

'Get myself a farm. Breed horses.'

'Won't that mean living in one place all the time?'

'I can camp out sometimes.'

'Are you all alone on this farm?'

'No, there's the horses.'

'You know what I mean, stop dodging the issue.'

'You mean have I tied myself down to a husband? No way. What for? Having some guy drive me nuts. Knowing I was driving him nuts.'

'That's not always how it works out,' Leo said, choosing his words carefully, because he'd often said the same, and it alarmed him to find himself defending the other side. 'People can actually get on well, for a long time. Sometimes they even love each other. No, really, they can.'

'Sure they do. At the start. Then she has a baby and her waistline goes, he gets bored and hits the bottle, she nags, he gets mad, she nags some more.'

'That's life in the foster homes speaking, is it?'

'One after another. Wherever it was—always the same. And you can keep it.'

'You don't believe people can ever love each other for life?'

Her face lit up with hilarity. 'Leo, you're a sentimentalist. You believe in that stuff.'

'I'm Italian,' he said evasively. 'We're supposed to believe in ''that stuff''.'

'No kidding! I'll bet you think moon rhymes with June, and love is for ever and a day. Oh, boy, you're priceless. Well, it's a better line than Paulie's.'

He didn't answer, and after a moment she was alerted by a new quality in the silence. Looking up, she saw Leo's eyes dark with anger. He met her puzzled gaze with one of fire.

'What did I say?' she asked.

'If you don't know the answer I can't tell you. But I'll try. You reckon I'm no better than Paulie, that I'm handing you a line prior to pawing you about in the stable. *Thanks*!'

'I didn't mean—'

'I think you did. Every man is the same in your eyes because you won't take the trouble to look up.'

He jumped to his feet and strode away from the stream to where the land rose sharply. At the top of the steep incline was a rock, and he scrabbled up there until he could sit on the top, staring angrily into space.

Selena glared at him in her dismay, furious with him, herself, the world. It hadn't occurred to her that she could hurt him. Her rough and tumble life had taught her directness but not subtlety. If you wanted something, you went for it, because nobody was going to give it to you. She had the tough skills of survival but not the gentle ones of beguilement, and for the first time it occurred to her that there was something missing in her armoury.

She scrambled up the incline until she was just below him, and was relieved to see that the anger had faded from his face. She didn't fear his anger, but it was his gentleness that was beginning to weave spells about her heart.

He reached down a hand to haul her up, so that she could sit down beside him.

'You're not really mad at me, are you?'

'Grrr!' he said, like a bear.

She chuckled, wrapping both arms around one of his and leaning her head against his shoulder.

'I'm sorry, Leo. I'm always like this. I open my big mouth first and think later.'

'You? Think?'

'I manage it sometimes.'

'You must send me a ticket. I'll bet it's quite an event.'

She freed a hand long enough to thump him, then put it back, and they sat contentedly together for a while.

He turned his head so that he could see as much of her face as was visible, and placed one of his big hands over her narrow one.

'I really didn't mean to lump you with Paulie,' she said. 'I should have known you're not like him, groping around, trying to sneak a kiss.'

Leo spoke quietly. 'I did not say I didn't want to kiss you.'

'What was that?' she asked quickly.

'Nothing.' This conversation was getting dangerous. He was too close to admitting what he really wanted, and shattering the delicate web of trust that was building up between them. And when he thought of what he would probably discover when they returned home he knew that web had to be protected at all costs.

'Perhaps it's time we went back,' he said.

They took the journey home easily as the sun slid down the sky. As they cantered back into the yard Leo exchanged a silent glance with Barton, and knew that their worst fears had been realised.

'She said it herself,' Barton told him, when Selena was out of earshot in the stable. 'They took one look at her van and roared with laughter. Oh, they'll pay for the damage, but only as a write-off. It won't buy her any replacements.'

'That settles it,' Leo said. 'It has to be Plan B.'

'I didn't know we even had a Plan A,' Barton said, startled.

'Plan A is the one that's just collapsed. Now, this is Plan B...'

He took Barton's arm and drew him well out of the way, so that all Selena heard from inside the stable, was Barton's roar of, *'Are you out of your mind?'*

CHAPTER FIVE

LEO not only meant to attend the rodeo in Stephenville, he was going to be a part of it. With what Barton called 'more nerve than common sense' he was determined to ride a bull.

'Just one bull,' he argued with Barton. 'What harm can it do?'

'Break your neck. That enough?'

They were at breakfast with the family, and since they were at opposite ends of the table the others began looking back and forth like spectators at a tennis match. Jack, who studied even at the table, took his nose out of his book long enough to begin scoring them.

'Barton I know what I'm doing,' Leo insisted.

'Fifteen love,' Jack intoned. 'Leo serving.'

'In a pig's ear you know what you're doing,' Barton retorted.

'Fifteen all.'

'It just takes practise.'

'Been doing that in Italy have you? First I knew they had bucking bulls out there. Does it say *Mama Mia!* as it throws you off?' Barton roared at his own joke.

'Fifteen thirty!'

'I just need to practise with your bucking machine.'

'And make it my fault? No way!'

'OK,' Leo sighed. 'I'll just have to enter without getting any practise, so when I break my neck, it *will* be your fault.'

'That's hitting below the belt,' Barton roared.

'Let him do it, Dad,' Carrie begged.

'You *want* him to get hurt? Thought you'd taken a shine to him.'

'*Dad!*' she hissed in an agony of embarrassment.

Selena had been enjoying the scene until then, but she pitied the girl, having her teenage crush exposed, and her misery compounded by a deep blush. Leo, she was sure, would pretend nothing had happened.

To her astonishment he did just the opposite.

'You see, I have a supporter,' he announced, pointing at Carrie. 'Carrie, you think I can do it, don't you?'

'Yes,' she said defiantly.

'And you don't think I'll break my neck?'

'I think you'll be great.'

'There you are, Barton. Listen to my friend over there. She knows what she's talking about.'

It was beautifully done, Selena had to admit that, watching Carrie's blush fade and her smile return. In a few seconds Leo had 're-packaged' her crush on him into a friendship he openly valued. It was clever, and it was kind.

Warmth and happiness pervaded her. She didn't know why Leo's kindness to someone else should give her that feeling. Yet it was like receiving a personal gift. The nicer he was than other men, the happier it made her.

Grumbling, Barton gave in, and after breakfast they all went out to his mechanical bull, an electrically driven machine, designed to be ridden, that bucked and tossed to give the rider some practise in hanging on for dear life. It had a range of speeds, starting with 'gentle' for beginners, and Barton, to Leo's disgust, insisted on setting it as low as possible.

With the whole family and Selena watching avidly Leo sailed through the first test. Encouraged, he raised the stakes, and still managed to hang on.

'Isn't he wonderful?' Carrie whispered to Selena. 'You'd never know he hadn't done it before.'

'Yes, you would,' Selena said with a grin.

'Well, you know what I mean.'

'Yes, I know,' Selena murmured so quietly that Carrie didn't hear her.

Jack had joined them, another book in his hand.

'Wanna know Leo's chance of getting killed the first time he—?'

'*No!*' they both said firmly.

A scream from Billie made them turn their heads sharply in time to see Leo flying through the air, to land with a crash, and lie still.

Carrie buried her face in her hands. 'I can't look. Is he all right?'

'I don't know,' Selena said in a voice that didn't sound like her own. 'He isn't moving.'

She had the horrible feeling that time had stopped as she began to run to where Leo lay. As she reached him he let out a hideous whooping sound. Again and again he made the dreadful noise and she felt time begin again as she recognised the symptoms of a man who'd had the breath knocked out of his body.

She dropped down beside him just as he managed to half raise himself. Still unable to speak, he clutched hold of her while the hoots and gasps came from him without end. Selena held onto him, knowing there was nothing to do until he'd struggled back to some sort of normality.

When the fit had passed he seemed exhausted, leaning against her and heaving. But then he looked up at the others who'd crowded around him, and gave his irrepressible grin.

'I told you I could do it,' he said.

From then on they were in countdown to the rodeo. The town was filling up, Barton entertained a constant stream of buyers who looked over his excellent horses, nodded and reached for their wallets. Delia, a great entertainer, was in her element, giving parties and overseeing the stock of cowboy clothes and memorabilia for the stall she would set up.

There was a strict dress code. Riders must wear a western hat, long-sleeved shirt and cowboy boots. Leo, who had none of these things, went to town among Delia's stock, kitting himself out both for now and for Grosseto when he returned home.

'They're going to think you're so fine,' Carrie said, regarding him admiringly in his new stetson and decorated boots.

'Nothing like a new hat to make an impression,' Leo said cheerfully. 'Let's see one on you.'

He settled a stetson on Carrie's head, then one on Billie's and finally on Selena's, nodded with satisfaction and took out his credit card.

'Delia, I'll have those three as well.'

In this way he contrived to buy Selena a present without offending her. He'd spent a lot of time working out how to do that.

Sometimes they practised together. If he did nothing else in his life he was determined to ride that bull.

On the face of it, it was simple. To stay eight seconds on the back of a heaving, thrashing mountain of furious bull. And live. That was the target.

'Think you'll do it?' she asked him one evening as they limped stiffly home.

'Do *you* think I will?'

'Nope.'

'Me neither. I don't care. I'm just doing it for fun. I'm no threat to anyone trying to earn a living.'

She grinned. 'That's true.'

'OK, OK, no need to rub it in.'

Leo had graduated from the bucking machine to Old Jim, a real live bull. The problem was that Jim had mellowed with age. He liked people, and he took an immediate shine to Leo, which was pleasant in its way but made him useless for practical purposes. Leo could manage eight seconds on Old Jim's back, but so could Selena. So, for that matter, could Delia, Billie and Carrie. And Jack.

Selena practised fiercely, racing around the barrels on Jeepers, aiming to keep their time down to fourteen seconds, or even under.

'Is that the "gold standard"?' Leo asked her.

'It is for here,' she said, indicating the barrels that Barton had set up. 'They're not the same in every rodeo. Sometimes they're further apart and that can be a seventeen-second circuit. But barrels at this distance should be fourteen seconds. Jeepers can do it. We're just not quite used to each other yet. I still make mistakes on him.'

As if to prove it she tried to take a corner too tightly and landed in the dust.

Leo, watching from a fence rail, started to race towards her, but she was up at once, leaping back into the saddle to try again, more carefully this time. Leo retreated.

'I thought you might have hurt yourself,' he said when she dismounted.

'Me?' she asked hilariously. 'With that little fall? I've had worse. I've probably got worse to come in the future. It's no big deal.'

He sighed. 'Couldn't you be frail and vulnerable sometimes, like other women?'

She hooted with laughter. 'Leo, what planet have you been living on? Women aren't frail and vulnerable these days.' She slapped him on the shoulder and every bone in his bruised body seemed to clang.

What could you do with a woman like this? he wondered. You couldn't say consoling things like 'Let me make it better,' because she'd think you were nuts and probably step on your toe, by way of bringing you to your senses.

You could only wait and hope, certain that the sweet kernel was in there, however well hidden by the prickly skin, knowing that what happened would be in her own good time, or not at all.

'Let's go and rub ourselves down with liniment,' she said.

'I'll do you if you'll do me,' he said hopefully.

She chuckled and thumped him again.

Barton was in his study that evening, watching for their return, and at his signal Leo halted Selena with the words, 'Come back outside, there's something I want you to see.'

In the yard stood a Mini Motor Home, functional rather than luxurious, but a palace compared to what Selena had originally driven. Attached to it was a horse trailer, plain but of good design.

'They're yours,' Barton said. 'To replace the ones you lost.'

'The insurers came through?' she breathed.

'The fact is,' Barton said with a hint of awkwardness, 'I don't really want to go to my insurers about this. I haven't had a claim in years, and if I make one now—well it would be cheaper if I just replace what I wrecked.'

'But—I don't get that,' Selena said. 'The damage to your car—it can't be cheaper than—'

'You just leave that to me,' Barton interrupted. 'It's cheaper because—that's how it works out.'

'But Barton—'

'Women don't understand these things,' Barton said desperately.

'I understand—'

'No, you don't, you don't understand anything. I've gone into it and—I don't want any more argument. You take Jeepers, you take the vehicles, and we call it quits.'

'You're—giving me these?' Selena asked, dazed. 'But I can't accept. My things weren't nearly as good—'

'But they got you from place to place OK,' Barton said. 'Well, this will get you from place to place as well.'

'I—'

'It's no more than your right,' Barton finished with a hunted look. He was running out of inspiration.

'But Jeepers—'

'He likes you. He works well for you. And the trailer will take two horses, so when Elliot's recovered you can take them both.'

'That won't be long now,' Selena said firmly.

'Sure it won't. But until then, Jeepers will keep you going.'

Leo watched them in silence. One thing they all knew, although she wasn't ready to admit it. Elliot's rodeo days were over.

He left Selena looking over her new home, and pounced on Barton halfway to the house.

'I thought you were going to blow everything,' he muttered.

'Not my fault. She was bound to be suspicious. I had to improvise.'

'"Women don't understand these things,"' Leo scoffed. 'No man dares say that these days, not if he wants to live.'

Barton turned on him.

'All right, you do better. Try telling her the truth. Tell her you're paying for everything, and see how she takes it.'

'Sssshh!' Leo said frantically. 'She mustn't know that. She'd skin me alive.'

'Great! Then we know where we are. Now are you gonna stand here yakking all night, or are you coming in the house for a whisky?'

'I'm coming in the house for a whisky.'

Everyone was up early on the first day of the rodeo. Delia and her daughters loaded piles of new stock into the truck. Barton checked off a list of contacts he was planning to do business with in a convivial atmosphere. Jeepers was groomed until he shone, and led out into the horse trailer.

Instinct sent Leo into the stables in search of Selena. He found her, as he'd expected, in Elliot's stall, caressing the horse's nose, murmuring tenderly.

'This isn't for good, you've got to understand that. Jeepers is a fine horse, but he's not you. It'll never be with him like it was with you and me. We're going to be together again. That's a promise.'

She rested her cheek against his nose. 'I love you, you ramshackle old brute. More than anyone in the world. Do you hear that?'

Leo tried to back out quietly, but he didn't quite manage it, and Selena looked up.

'Now who's being sentimental?' he asked kindly.

'I am not. I'm just thinking of his feelings. Have you thought what it must be like for him to see another horse being groomed and led out for me to ride, in his place? Do you think he doesn't know?'

'I guess he knows everything you're thinking.'

'And I know everything he's thinking.'

'Well, what are you going to tell him if you win?'

She whirled on him, an almost painful intensity in her face. 'Leo, do you think I might win?'

'Does it really mean that much?' he asked, studying her face as though hoping to find something there.

'It means everything. I have to make some money to keep going onto the next rodeo, and the next. It's my whole life, *everything*.'

'Well, if you don't I could always—' he stopped because her fingertips were over his mouth.

'Don't say it. I don't take charity and I won't take money from you.'

He maintained a diplomatic silence. This was no time to tell her how much he'd already given her.

'After all, why should you take financial risks for me?' she went on. 'Suppose I couldn't pay it back? Where would you be?'

'Selena, I'm not at my last gasp, like you. What's wrong with letting a friend help you? There's no law that says you have to be independent all the time.'

'Yes there is. I passed one. It's my law, the one I live by, and I can't change. I do it myself or no deal.'

'Selena, it's not weakness to accept help.'

'No, but it's weakness to rely on it. You become weak by believing that someone'll always be there for you. Because sooner or later, they won't.'

He frowned. 'If you really believe that, heaven help you!'

'Leo, why are we quarrelling? It's a wonderful day. We're going to have a great time, and I'm going to win. I can't lose.'

He regarded her with his head on one side. 'Why can't you lose?'

'Because I got my miracle. You know when we met on the highway?'

'Met isn't quite the word I'd have used, but go on.'

'Before that I'd been with Ben, he's an old friend and he was fixing my van. He said I needed a miracle or a millionaire, but I said forget millionaires. They're not good for anything.'

'So you settled for a miracle?' Leo asked, feeling the beginnings of a smile somewhere inside him.

'Right. I said I just knew my miracle was on its way to me.'

The smile grew bigger. 'And it was?'

'You know it was. All the time Barton was on the highway, and we were fated to meet.'

The smile faded. 'Barton?'

'Well, wasn't it a miracle that he turned out to be a good man with a conscience, who didn't duck his obligations, as a lot of them would have?'

'But a millionaire, don't forget,' Leo quibbled.

'Ah, well, there must be one or two good ones. The point is, he was nice about it, which just proves what a decent man he is.'

'Right,' Leo said in a hollow voice.

'So I got my miracle. And now I'm going to win.'

'So am I. All right, stop laughing.' Selena had doubled up. 'I can do eight seconds on Old Jim, you saw me yesterday.'

'Sure, and I've also seen him accepting tidbits from your hand. Old Jim is a pussy cat. You won't be riding him in the ring.' She got out of range and added wickedly, 'You won't be riding anything for very long.'

'Now there's a thing. I thought we were friends, and you hurt my feelings like that.'

At once she came back into range, putting her hands on either side of his head, full of contrition.

'Leo, I'm so sorry. I didn't mean to hurt you after you've been good to me. It was just a joke—'

'Hell, I knew that.'

'Are you sure? I can be a bitch sometimes. I don't mean to be, but that doesn't stop me.'

Leo, who knew a thing or two about doing things he hadn't meant to do ten seconds earlier, nodded in perfect understanding.

'Say you're not really hurt,' she pleaded. 'You're my best friend and if you get mad at me, I'd really hate it.'

Leo let his arms slip around her waist. His feelings weren't hurt at all, but he managed to regard her sadly, while silencing his conscience. He couldn't be blamed for making the most of this, could he?

'I'm not mad,' he said bravely.

'You're not hurt either, are you?' she demanded, reading him without trouble. But she didn't move her hands, except to slide them behind his neck. Nor did she resist when he drew her closer.

'Stricken to the heart, I promise,' he said.

She didn't answer, but stood there gazing into his face, while mischief danced over her face, her eyes, her smiling lips.

'Selena,' he said unsteadily, 'you are putting me under a lot of strain here.'

'You think I ought to do something about that?'

'Yes, I really do.'

She tilted her head in a way that made his heart do somersaults.

'Well, I got tired of waiting for you to do something about it,' she said as she laid her lips on his.

They were just as he'd imagined them, sweet and enticing, yet with a hint of something underneath that wasn't sweet at all: spicy, challenging, hot as a pepper. Not an *ingénue*, but a woman of determination, ready to take him on.

Selena's head was whirling. She hadn't meant to do this, but there was something she needed to know, and suddenly her impatience had become too much to bear. Laying her mouth against his was an act of exploration and defiance in equal measure.

She knew at once that she would have done better to wait. No woman, with a busy day ahead, could afford this kind of distraction. And she had only herself to blame because she'd always known that this man would take all of a woman's attention. Some pleasures weren't to be skimped.

He seemed to feel the same because he slid his arms about her with a gentleness that didn't disguise their power. She wanted to know all about that power. She could feel it in his lips, testing hers cautiously to divine her true meaning, then seeming to think he understood and coming on strongly in a way that excited her.

She mustn't do this, she thought dizzily. Her timing was dreadful.

'Leo—'

'Yes—'

From outside came Barton's bellow. 'Anyone in there? We're ready to go.'

Leo released her, groaning. 'I like Barton, but—'

Selena came back to earth and the realisation that she'd nearly thrown everything away for this man. With a great effort she pulled herself together, saying urgently, 'No, he's right. We have to stop this.'

'We do?'

'It—it wastes vital energy.' She could feel her vital energy being sapped just by being this close to him.

'I didn't think it was a waste.'

'There'll be time later. For now we've got to psych ourselves up for the big day. Shoulders back, head up. Believe in yourself.'

'I find it easier to believe in you. You're going to win. You've got Jeepers down to fourteen seconds, which I never thought you'd do.'

She danced with excitement. 'I knew he could do it, he is such a fantastic horse, so fast and strong—'

'Careful! You said that in front of Elliot! You could give him a complex.'

'Oh—*you*!'

She thumped him, he put his arm about her shoulders and they went out, laughing, together.

CHAPTER SIX

REACHING the rodeo site was like entering a village. There was the arena where the events took place, the area where the horses were delivered and kept until ready, and the shopping mall where Delia and dozens of others set out their stalls.

Leo had driven to the arena with Selena and together they delivered Jeepers to his stall. When he was settled they headed for Delia's stall and Leo promptly embarked on another spending spree.

'Who are they for?' Selena asked as he paid for a pair of extremely glamorous and impractical spurs.

'My cousin Marco.' Leo grinned. 'Never sat on a horse in his life. They'll really annoy him.'

'You're wicked in your own way, y'know that?'

'Proud of it. Now this—' he held up a figure of a cowboy on horseback made of painted stone. It was exquisite, full of life. 'This is for my brother Guido,' he said. 'He sells souvenirs in Venice. This'll show him how it's done.'

'What kind of souvenirs?'

'Venetian masks mostly. And gondola lamps. They go on top of television sets. Some of them play ''O sole mio'' when you switch them on.'

'You're kidding me!'

'Nope.'

'Well, you shouldn't be hard on a man trying to earn a living.'

'He—certainly—does very well out of souvenirs,' Leo said cautiously. 'Perhaps it's time we were going. They'll be starting soon.'

Leo had arranged to do his bull riding on the first day, in order to 'get the disaster over fast,' Selena had cheekily observed.

As he'd expected, there was a great deal of difference between Old Jim and the huge, furious animal he encountered now. Nothing in the previous few days with the machine had prepared him for it. It felt as though the bull had personally decided to smash him to fragments as a punishment for his impertinence in even trying.

And he must try to endure this for eight seconds, he thought fuzzily as his brain was bounced around in his skull.

But it was a considerate bull.

It had him off him in three.

He landed hard but he survived. By that time he was getting good at falling off, having had so much practise.

As he limped out of the ring he heard the kindly applause of the crowd, a tribute to his guts at doing something he was so hopelessly bad at, and saw the Hanworths clapping for him with the warmth of friends. All except Paulie whose sneer of pleasure was unmistakable.

But Selena wasn't sneering. Her eyes were bright with pleasure that he'd made the attempt, and her smile was a promise and a reminder. Leo grinned back at her, happy and content. Paulie could go stuff himself up a drainpipe!

Behind her smile Selena felt wrung out. When Leo had gone flying over the bull's head she'd ground her nails into her palm until he picked himself up. He hadn't broken his neck. He was alive. The world could start again.

She chided herself for making a fuss about nothing. How many men had she seen thrown? But none of them had been Leo.

She slipped away to get ready. Jeepers was there, calmly waiting for her. They'd done well together in the practise ring, but this was different. This was opening night. She adjusted her stetson, making sure it was firmly fixed on. Losing a hat could cost valuable points. Not as many as knocking over a barrel, but enough to do damage.

There were five riders going before her, and they all did well.

'All right,' she told Jeepers. 'The trick is not to let them scare you. You're—*we're* as good as they are. C'mon boy! Let's show 'em.'

As the bell rang she went flying over the starting line heading for the first barrel inside the triangle, a sharp turn, but not too sharp, allowing Jeepers space to move. They were around, then on to the next, neat turn, on to the last, then over the finishing line to cheers as the clock showed her in the lead.

Leo was waiting for her just out of the ring and together they watched the next rider.

'She's not a patch on you,' he said loyally. 'None of them are.'

'The next one's good though. Jan Dennem. I've raced against her a lot and she's always been just ahead of me.'

'This time you'll beat her,' he said confidently.

They held their breaths while fourteen interminable seconds ticked away and Jan swept across the line one-tenth of a second outside Selena's time.

'Yeeee-eeess!' they roared from the sanctuary of each other's arms.

Next competitor. Very fast. A real threat. Ahead of Selena by half a second as she approached the final barrel, but then—

A roar went up from the crowd as the barrel was knocked over.

The next two were slower. No question. Selena was still ahead.

'One more,' she said. 'I can't bear it. Leo?'

When he didn't answer she looked and found him standing with the fingers of both hands crossed, his eyes closed, his lips moving.

'Just praying,' he said when he'd opened his eyes. 'You never know.'

She gave a shaky laugh. 'Does God follow the rodeo?'

'Never misses.'

There was a cheer as the last competitor came flying out into the ring.

'I can't look,' Selena said, and buried her face against Leo's chest. At once he put his arms about her. 'What's happening?'

'First barrel, she's fast but you're all right, second barrel—now the third—'

The crowd's cheers became deafening. Leo groaned as he tightened his arms and rested his head on hers.

'Oh, no!' she cried. 'No, no, no!'

'By a tenth of a second,' Leo said. 'I'm sorry *carissima*.'

She raised her head. 'What did you call me?'

'*Carissima*. It's Italian.'

'Yes, but what does it mean?'

'Well—'

But while he wondered whether to risk telling her that the word meant 'Darling' they heard a bellow from Barton, congratulating and commiserating with her both together.

The moment passed, and Leo was left reflecting that he who hesitated was lost. Or if not actually lost, then forced to wait for another chance.

It was a cheerful party that drove home that night. Delia had done excellent business, Selena had picked up some prize money for coming second, and Leo had stayed on the bull for a whole three seconds. That was cause for rejoicing, so they did, far into the night.

Despite her defeat Selena was happy. The money for second had been better than usual. Leo found her sitting on the porch, contemplating it blissfully.

'I'm rich, I'm rich!'

'A hundred dollars is rich?' he asked quizzically.

'It's a king's ransom. Well, OK, maybe a very minor king. Who wants to ransom a king anyway? Do away with the lot!'

She was drunk with her little bit of success, laughing as she talked, going wildly, joyfully over the top.

'So much for royalty,' Leo observed. 'Obviously you don't believe in them.'

'Who needs 'em? Or guys with handles.'

'You mean titles?' he asked, sensing the conversation taking a dangerous turn. 'Down with the wicked aristocrats? Ouch!' He rubbed his shoulder.

'What's the matter?' she asked quickly. 'You got a neck pain, shoulder pain?'

'More of a whole body pain,' he said ruefully. 'But perhaps the neck more than the rest.'

'Here, let me have a go,' she said, getting behind him and rubbing his neck. 'This is no good. Your collar's in the way. Take your shirt off.'

She helped him off with it, then got to work on his neck, his shoulders, his spine, with deft, skilful fingers.

'Thanks,' he said gratefully. 'Hey, you're good at this.'

'I do it a lot.'

'You do this for all the guys? Aren't there medical people whose job it is?'

'Sure, but if you can't afford them you do it for each other.'

He considered this, not liking the implications. But her fingers were spreading welcome warmth and ease, and he settled for counting his blessings.

'You've got them in Italy, haven't you?' she asked.

'What?'

'Aristocrats. Careful, don't jump like that or I might hurt you.'

'Did I? Didn't mean to.' The word aristocrats had caught him by surprise.

'Italy is a republic—but we've still got one or two of them,' he said cautiously.

'Ever actually met them, I mean talked to them, face to face?'

'They're not a species of reptile, Selena.'

'That's just what they are. They should be in a cage in a zoo.'

'But you know nothing about them.'

'Well, do you?'

'I know that some of them aren't so bad.'

'Why are you defending them? You should be on my side—down the aristos, up the workers.'

'So you'd like to send them all to the guillotine?'

She shook her head. 'No, I'd make them get their hands dirty in the fields, with the workers, like us.'

'You don't know I'm a worker,' he said. 'Who knows what I do when I'm back in Italy?'

She left what she was doing and took one of his hands in hers. It was large and roughened.

'Of course I know,' she said. 'This is a worker's hand. It's been battered and hurt a few times. It's got scars.'

It was all true, but the fields were his own and they brought him a fortune larger than Barton's. His innocent deception lay heavy on him, and suddenly he couldn't bear it.

'Selena—'

She didn't seem to hear him. She was turning his hand over, holding it gently. Then she looked up and her gaze shocked him with its innocent candour. There was a glow in her eyes that seemed to dazzle him, and he looked quickly away.

'What is it?' she asked quietly, laying down his hand.

'Nothing, I—' He gave her a bright, forced smile, and spoke hurriedly. 'I'm just aching all over. Tomorrow I'll see a bone-setter. Well, now, I reckon it's time to turn in. You too. You've had a long, hard day.'

'Yes, I have,' she murmured bleakly. 'Very hard.'

The last night of the rodeo was to be marked by one of the barbecues that Barton gave at the drop of a hat. There was no hospitality like that to be found at the Four-Ten, and as they drove back they were followed by a procession of vehicles.

Leo knew a curious sense of dissatisfaction. He would be leaving next day, but he wasn't ready for that. Something had started here but not finished, and he couldn't make things happen because he didn't know enough about his own feelings.

Selena tugged at his heart as no other woman had ever done, but there were chasms between them, chasms of lifestyle, country, language. They didn't even believe in the same kind of future. Only the most overwhelming love could overcome such problems. And how could he hope for such love from a woman who seemed not to believe in it?

The thought of saying goodbye hurt badly. He'd hoped she minded as much, but she made it impossible to tell. And perhaps that was his answer.

They'd seen little of each other since the night she'd rubbed his back and he'd nearly been overwhelmed by his longing for her, and his conscience-stricken awareness that he was treading a fine line.

The next day he'd been to a chiropractor, who pulled and pushed him, told him not to be such a darned fool another time, and left him a hundred dollars poorer. He'd still ached afterward, although whether it was from the fall or the treatment he couldn't say, but he felt a good deal better now.

He dressed quickly for the evening. From down below came the sounds of music and laughter and he looked out on the pleasant scene. Sweet-smelling smoke came from the barbecue, lights were strung between the trees and the music seemed to beckon him.

Selena was already there. He could see her in the centre of a small crowd, and guessed she'd done herself some good with her fizzing performances. Her future would be brighter now, and the help he'd given her would bear fruit, even if she didn't know it; even if she forgot about him completely and never gave him another thought for the rest of her days.

On that gloomy reflection he went down to join the party.

There was plenty to distract him, great food, fine whisky, smiling ladies. But suddenly his appetite had gone and he didn't want to drink. He followed her jealously with his eyes, dancing when he had to, but always trying to keep her in view.

Barton, good host that he was, made much of his guests, calling for toasts and rounds of applause. Leo joined in the applause for Selena and raised his glass to her. She raised hers back.

As everyone broke into another boisterous dance he made his way through the crowd to her and saw that her eyes were shining.

'I feel so good,' she said happily. 'Oh, Leo, if you only knew how good I feel!'

'That's great,' he said tenderly. 'That's how I always want you to feel.'

'I've just been interviewed by the local paper about my "successes"—both of them.'

After being narrowly beaten in the first barrel race, she'd won on the following day, and achieved another second on the day after. On the final day there had been a big event for the best ten competitors from the previous races. And she'd stormed to victory.

'Do you know how much money I've got now?' she asked in wonder.

'Yes, I do. You told me. And take care of it.'

'It's more than I've ever had before at one time.'

'What are you going to do with it?'

'Enter more events. This could see me through my next six months.'

'And then?'

'By then I should have enough for the next year. I'm on my way.'

Which didn't sound much as if she was planning to pine for him.

He chinked glasses with her, then walked away to sweep Carrie into the mêlée. They danced until they were both breathless and laughing, then went into the waltz together.

'Did you manage it?' Carrie asked.

'It?'

'Selena. Is she as nuts about you as you are about her?' Since the day Leo had appealed to her in the discussion about bull riding she'd settled into the role of the understanding sister.

'She sure isn't nuts about me.'

'But you are about her.'

'Carrie, please!'

'OK. Only I think I saw her looking for you, and I was planning to melt tactfully away, but if—'

'You're a darling.'

He kissed her cheek and turned to find Selena eyeing him with a curious little smile on her lips.

'You haven't danced with me yet,' she said.

Carrie melted, as promised, only taking a quick look back to see Leo and Selena go into each other's arms like two halves of a whole.

They danced in silence for a while, each thinking that by this time tomorrow they would have gone their separate ways.

Selena was full of confusion. She'd said goodbyes before, but never like this. She tried to be practical. All she had to do was hold out until he'd gone, and then forget him. It should be easy forgetting a man half a world away. But her heart was telling her that he would never be far away from her again, because she would carry him with her every moment, for the rest of her life.

The music changed. Suddenly a lone violin was playing a melancholy strain of longing and farewell. She would never see him again. She held him close and her heart ached.

With her eyes closed, she didn't see where he was taking her. She only knew that they were dancing, circling, circling, while the sounds faded. She danced on in a dream where there was only herself and him, circling around and around.

'Selena…'

His voice whispering her name made her open her eyes to find his face close to hers.

'Selena,' he said again, his breath brushing her face, and her murmured, 'Yes,' was so swift that their breath intermingled.

Then his mouth was on hers, and he was kissing her with a fierceness born out of desperation. She was slipping through his fingers, and holding her was like trying to hold onto quicksilver.

She answered him with the same fierceness. From the moment they'd met something had been bound to happen between them, and it had taken too long. Now she wouldn't let it go. She would have her hour, whatever it cost, and live in its glory all her days.

Her life had taught her little about love and tenderness. What she knew she'd discovered for herself. Something was happening inside her now that was totally new. She hadn't known before that just being in a man's arms could make her ache with joy and sadness together, so that she didn't know which one was the greater. Nor did it matter. She was alive to feelings and sensations that she would never regret, no matter how much pain they might cost her. And there would be pain. Life had taught her that much.

She'd kissed other men, but none like this. He was a man whom, she guessed, had lived a full life with women, yet his touch had a curious innocence about it, as though he too was experiencing something for the first time. Through the driving urgency she could still feel the tenderness, as though caring for her mattered more to him than any other satisfaction.

Yet he wanted her to the point where it was driving him crazy. She could sense that through the trembling of his great, powerful body, the rise and fall of his chest. It excited her to know that she affected him so much. She wanted him as much in thrall to her as she was to him, and she teased him with her lips, urging him on to the point where they would meet.

It was he who ended the kiss, seizing her shoulders and pushing her back a few inches, so that he could look into her face. His own was wild.

'We picked one heckuva time,' he gasped. 'Maybe we should—'

'Maybe we should what? Be sensible? Who wants to be sensible?'

'Well I sure don't, but you—Selena, tomorrow—' He stopped. The words of cool wisdom hung in the air and died unspoken.

'Yes,' she whispered. 'Yes—'

From somewhere in the background a sound was growing closer. Cheering, laughing, singing, cheerful guests in the last yell of enjoyment before the party began to break up. Leo looked desperately to where light and noise were streaming towards him, engulfing him.

'Hey, look who's hiding himself under the trees!'

'Who is she, Leo?'

He laughed loudly, trying to brush it off. Someone pressed a drink on him and he took it. Everyone was kissing everyone.

When he looked around for Selena she had gone.

It seemed an age before the goodnights were said, but at last the place was quiet and Leo could draw a long breath. Perhaps they could still have a moment alone together, and answer some of the questions that had been raised under the trees.

But there was no sign of Selena. So many promises in her kiss, and she'd just left him.

He made his way up to bed, frowning, trying to see a way through the confusion. Hell would freeze over before he would go knocking on her door. The next move had to be hers.

So he told himself. But he still went to her door and knocked softly. It was that or spend the rest of his life wondering. Getting no reply he knocked a little louder, and waited. Still no reply.

He went to his own room. At the window he looked out on the dark landscape, knowing it had been foolish to indulge in dreams when he was leaving tomorrow. Whatever happened now was too late. He stood there, telling himself it was best to be sensible, and trying to believe it.

He didn't know what made him aware that he wasn't alone in the room. It wasn't even as definite as the sound of breathing, but something changed in the atmosphere, and when he stretched out his hand to the lamp a voice in the darkness whispered, 'Don't put on the light.'

'Where are you?' he said.

She didn't answer, but the next moment two soft arms were around his neck, and a slim, naked body was pressed against his.

'You were here all the time?' he asked. 'I just got back from—'

'I know, I heard you.' Her chuckle delighted him.

He'd remembered her from the first day as a gazelle, a nymph, so delicately built was she. Now in the darkness his hands discovered what his eyes had known, and found the beauty he'd dreamed of since that moment.

Her fingers were working on his shirt, opening the buttons, finding his chest, the slight rise and fall of his muscles, sliding her palms over them.

'If you don't mean to follow through, you're doing something very dangerous,' Leo groaned.

'I never start what I don't mean to finish,' she murmured so that her breath fanned his face.

She was easing his shirt down his arms as she spoke, inch by inch until he couldn't stand it any more and wrenched it off. Then he could pull her against him, revelling in the feel of her soft skin against his own. He closed his eyes, wondering how anything could feel so good and still leave him standing.

He stripped off the rest of his clothes as fast as he could. This had been too long in coming to waste any time. Holding onto each other they made their way to the bed and collapsed on it so that he fell on his back with her on top of him.

'Remember when we were like this before?' she asked.

'The first day—I got you out of the bath—how can I forget?'

'We didn't end up like this though.'

'We would have done if I'd had anything to do with it,' he growled.

'Me too.'

'As soon as that?'

'As soon as that.'

She was laughing like a siren who'd finally enticed her prey into her circle, and that was fine by him. He'd happily be the prey, or anything, as long it led to this.

His hands were all over her, enjoying her lithe strength, her fluid movements, and what she was doing to him.

'I thought you were stiff and bruised,' she teased.

'My energy's coming back by the minute.'

She began covering him with kisses. She seemed to know him already, understanding by instinct the little caresses that drove him wild. When Leo slowly sat up, holding her in his lap, her fingers immediately found the place on the back of his neck where the lightest touch could reduce him to shivers. From there it was just a matter of time before she discovered how vulnerable his spine was as well.

'Witch,' he growled.

'Hmm!'

Suddenly he could stand it no longer. With a deep laugh he rolled over, tossing her onto her back with him on top of her.

'I've been thinking about this until I nearly went crazy,' he groaned.

Her whisper went through him like electricity. 'Why did we waste so much time?'

'Who cares?' he said. 'As long as we don't waste any more.'

He kissed her everywhere, celebrating her breasts, her tiny waist, her long, slim legs. She was quickly ready for him, telling him wordlessly of her eagerness, and when he entered her she gave a sigh of fulfilment.

His loving was like himself, robust and full-hearted, short on subtlety but long on warmth and generosity, giving more than he took. His slow movements increased her pleasure, driving it forward, harder, more intense, beautiful, ecstatic. He had the control to hold back, giving her every last moment before letting himself go.

And then it was like nothing in the world had ever been or ever would be again. Just for a few moments. Not long enough. She wanted so much more, and she would never stop wanting him. She knew, even as she felt her heartbeat slow to contentment, that he could start it racing again with a word.

They shared a glance, eyes gleaming in the dark, and suddenly they clutched each other, not in passion this time but in joyous mirth. For it was the biggest and most exhilarating joke in the whole world. Arms about each other's necks, they roared with laughter, knowing the joke was on them.

And then it wasn't funny any more, but only beautiful and fulfilling, and they were no longer themselves, but something entirely different called 'us'.

And tomorrow they were saying goodbye.

She'd known that Leo was a dangerously lovable man, but she was never more sure of it than when sex was over and he turned towards her, enfolding her in his arms and resting his face against her warm flesh, as though he needed more from her than physical pleasure.

That was a real dirty trick, she thought. How was a girl supposed to keep her independence of spirit with a man who behaved like that?

But when she was quite sure he was asleep she put her own arms around him, as far as she could, and stroked his hair, and kissed him again and again in a passion of tenderness and farewell.

CHAPTER SEVEN

THE worst thing about airports was having to arrive early, so that the goodbyes stretched out painfully. It was worse, Selena thought, if you were waiting for the other person to say something and you weren't sure what. And whatever it was, he didn't say it.

She drove him to Dallas Airport. They checked the time of the Atlanta flight, sent his luggage on its way, and found a coffee bar. But suddenly Leo jumped up and said, 'Come with me.'

'Where are we going?' she asked as he grasped her hand and hurried her away.

'I want to buy you a present before I go, and I've just realised what it should be.'

He led her to a shop that sold mobile phones. 'Anyone who moves around as much as you needs one of these,' he said.

'Couldn't afford it before.' She was briefly happy at this sign that he wanted to keep in touch. But no happiness could survive the reflection that he was going away, and she might never see him again.

They chose the phone together, and he bought the first thirty hours. She scribbled the number on a small piece of paper and watched as he tucked it away in his wallet.

'Time I was going through Passport Control.'

'Not just yet,' she said quickly. 'We've got time for another coffee.'

She had a terrifying feeling that everything was rushing to the edge of a precipice. She was the only one who could stop it, but she didn't know how. She couldn't manage the words, had never spoken them, barely knew them.

She'd done all she could to show him how she felt the night before. Now her heart was breaking, and she could only wonder that he seemed oblivious.

She spent the last few minutes drinking in the sight of him, trying to remember every line, every intonation of his voice.

He was going away. He would forget her.

She had never smiled so brightly.

'Will passengers—?'

'I guess that's it,' Leo said, getting to his feet.

She came with him almost to the gate. He stopped and touched her face gently.

'I wouldn't have missed this for the world,' he said.

'Oh, yeah?' she said lightly, and aimed a punch at his arm. 'You'll forget me as soon as the hostess flutters her eyelashes at you.'

But he didn't smile back. 'I'll never forget you, Selena.'

His face seemed to constrict and she thought for a moment that he would say something more. She waited, her heart beating with wild hope, but he only leaned down and kissed her cheek.

'Don't you forget me,' he said.

'Better call that number and make sure I don't.'

'I'll do that.'

He kissed her again before walking off. Try as she might she couldn't find in those kisses any echo of the night before when he'd kissed her in a very different way. Then he'd been a man thinking only of a woman, absorbed only in her, giving and receiving pleasure, and not only pleasure: tenderness and affection. Now he was a man who wanted to go home.

At the gate he turned and waved to her. She waved back, keeping a smile on her face by sheer force of will.

Then he was gone.

She didn't leave at once, as she'd meant to. Instead she waited by the window until the flight took off, and watched until the sky swallowed it up.

Then she walked back to the parking lot and got behind the wheel, talking to herself like a Dutch uncle.

What the heck! They were ships that passed in the night, and they'd passed. That was all. Ahead of her stretched a brighter future than she'd ever known. That was what she should be thinking of.

She slammed her hand down on the wheel. She'd never told herself pretty lies before.

But now she needed a comforting lie to get her over this moment.

'I should have said something,' she raged. 'Said anything, so he'd know. Then he might even have asked me to go with him. Oh, who am I fooling? He could have asked me to go, but he never thought of it. He won't call. That phone was a goodbye present. Stop being a fool Selena. You can't cry in a parking lot.'

The Atlanta/Pisa flight seemed to go on for ever, into not just another day, but another dimension, another world. Leo tried to sleep but couldn't. He left the aircraft, dazed with weariness and yawned his way through Passport Control and customs. It felt strange to be back in his own country.

He headed for the taxi rank, so absorbed in calculating how long it would take him to get home that he had no attention for the sounds of someone behind him. He didn't see what hit him, or how many of them there were, although witnesses later attested to four. He only knew that suddenly he was on the ground, being swarmed over by strangers.

Shouts, the sound of running. He sat up, feeling his head, wondering why there were so many policemen around. Hands helped him stagger to his feet.

'What happened?' he demanded.

'You were robbed, *signore*.'

He groaned and felt for the place where his wallet should have been. It was empty. His head was aching too much for him to think any further than this. Somebody called an ambulance and he was taken to the local hospital.

He awoke next morning to find a policeman by his bed, holding the missing wallet.

'We found it in an alley,' he said.

As expected, the wallet was empty. Money, credit cards were all gone. But what really appalled Leo was the fact that the slip of paper with Selena's number had also vanished.

Renzo, his overseer, collected him from the hospital and drove him the fifty miles home to Bella Podena. As soon as he found himself among the rolling hills of Tuscany Leo began to relax. Whatever the surface turmoil of his life, his instincts were telling him that what really mattered was to be home, where his vines grew and his fields of wheat lay under a benevolent sun.

He was popular with his employees because he paid them generously, trusted them and let them get on with their jobs. For the last lap of the journey they waved and yelled to him, glad to see him back.

The Calvani lands were extensive. For the last few miles he was looking at his own fields, and even his own village. Morenza, a tiny community of medieval buildings, stood on Calvani land, at the foot of the incline that led up to Leo's house. Its high street curved around the church, and a small duck pond, before leading out of the village and up through vines planted on the slope to catch the sun.

There at the top was the farmhouse, also medieval, made of stone, with a magnificent view down the valley. He entered it with a sigh of satisfaction, dropping his bags onto the floor and looking around him at the familiar things he loved.

There was Gina, with his favourite dish, already prepared and ready to serve. His favourite wine was at exactly the right temperature. His favourite dogs swarmed around his feet.

He ate a huge meal, kissed Gina on the cheek in thanks, and went to the room he used as a study, and from which he ran his estate. A couple of hours with Enrico, the assistant who supervised the paperwork during his absence, showed him that Enrico could manage this side of things perfectly well without him. He asked no more. The next day he would go over the land with men as close to the earth as himself.

He spent the next couple of hours on the telephone to his family, catching up on the news. Finally he went out and stood with a glass of wine, gazing down to the village, where the lights were coming on. He stood for a long time, listening to the breeze in the trees and the sound of bells echoing across the valley, and thought that he had never known such peace and beauty. And yet…

It was the perfect homecoming to the perfect place. But suddenly he felt alone as he had never done in his life before.

He went to bed and tried to sleep, but it was useless, and he got up and went downstairs to the study. In Texas it was early morning. It was Barton who answered.

'Selena isn't still there by any chance?' he asked hopefully.

'No, she left straight after you did. Just drove back here, collected Jeepers, and headed off. Didn't she do great? Jeepers was just the horse she needed. She's going to be a star with that animal.'

'Great. Great.' Leo tried to sound cheerful, but for a reason he didn't want to explore he wasn't pleased to hear of her success a world away. 'Has she called you at all?'

'Called yesterday to ask after Elliot. I told her he was doing fine.'

'Did she ask after me?' He'd promised himself not to ask that, but it came out anyway.

'No, she never mentioned you. But I'm sure if you called her—'

Why the devil should I call her if she doesn't care enough about me to ask? he thought.

'Barton, I can't call her. I got mugged and lost the paper with her mobile phone number. Can you let me have it?'

'I would if I had it myself. I wouldn't know how to contact her.'

'Next time she calls, will you explain and get her to call me?'

'Sure thing.'

'Did she tell you where she was going?'

'Reno—I think.'

'I'll leave a message for her there.'

He tried to concentrate on his coming visit to Venice, for the wedding of his younger half-brother, Guido, to his English fiancée, Dulcie. There would be another wedding the day before, when his uncle, Count Francesco Calvani, would marry Liza, his one-time housekeeper and the love of his life. That ceremony would be small and private.

He'd been looking forward to a cheerful family occasion, but now, suddenly, he didn't have the heart for weddings.

Where was she? Why didn't she contact him? Had she forgotten their night together so easily?

He sent emails to the rodeo web site at Reno, detailing his movements over the coming days, giving the phone number of his uncle's home in Venice and his own mobile. For good measure he reminded her of his home number.

To the last minute he clung to the hope that she would telephone him. But the phone remained silent, and at last he left for Venice.

*   *   *

Leo had never been a man to brood. It was rare for a woman to pass out of his life against his will, but if it happened he'd always been positive. The world was full of laughing ladies, as easygoing as himself, with whom he could pass the time. Suddenly, that thought brought him no cheer.

He took the train from Florence to Venice, where there was a family motor boat waiting to convey him to the Palazzo Calvani on the Grand Canal. He arrived to find the family at supper. He kissed Liza, then his uncle, then Dulcie, Harriet, and Lucia, Marco's mother. Guido was there too, and his cousin Marco. When he'd thumped them and been thumped back, the greetings were complete.

As he ate he tried to seem his normal self, and maybe he fooled his male relatives. But the women had sharper eyes, and when the meal was over Dulcie and Harriet corralled him onto the sofa like a pair of eager sheep dogs herding a lion, and settled one each side of him.

'You've found her at last,' Harriet said.

'Her?' he asked uneasily.

'You know what I mean. *Her*! The one. She's got you roped and tied.'

'What's her name?' Dulcie demanded.

He gave up stalling. He wasn't kidding them. 'She's called Selena,' he admitted. I met her in Texas. We were both in the rodeo.' He fell silent.

'And?' they asked eagerly. *'And?'*

'She fell off. So did I.'

'So you had something in common,' Dulcie said, nodding.

'A marriage of true minds,' Harriet agreed.

'I shouldn't think minds had much to do with it,' Dulcie suggested.

'Nothing at all,' Leo said, remembering Selena's sweetness, the tensile strength in her slim body, like spun steel, yet feeling so delicate in his hands. For a moment her hot breath seemed to whisper against his skin, inciting him to ever greater passion and tenderness.

'It was wonderful,' he said abruptly.

'You should have brought her here to meet us,' Harriet told him.

'That's just the trouble, I don't know where to find her.'

'But didn't you exchange names and addresses?' Dulcie asked.

'She doesn't have an address. She drives around the rodeos and lives wherever she is. I had her mobile phone number, but—well, if you must know someone stole my wallet, with the paper. I've tried to track her down over the internet, but for some reason I always seem to miss her. I might never see her again.'

The two young women made sympathetic noises, but Leo suspected they secretly found it rather funny. Perhaps it was. Leo Calvani, stallion and free spirit, off his feed because one young woman, with a prickly temper and no figure to speak of, had vanished. Hilarious.

After a while he joined the other men, but even their company couldn't soothe him. Two blissful bridegrooms and a fiancé weren't what he needed in his present disconsolate mood.

Gradually the party broke up. Guido and Dulcie disappeared together to enjoy the sweet nothings of a soon-to-be married couple. Marco and Harriet went off to stroll the streets of Venice. Leo went out into the garden, where he found his Aunt Lucia sitting peacefully, gazing up at the stars.

'I suppose Marco and Harriet will be setting the date at any moment,' Leo said, sitting down with her.

'I do hope so,' Lucia said eagerly. 'I know they've gone off together now, so maybe they'll come back with it all settled.'

'You're very keen on this marriage, aren't you?' he asked curiously. 'Even though—well, it's not exactly a love match, is it?'

'You mean I arranged it? Yes, I did, I don't deny it.'

'Wouldn't it have been safer to let him pick his own bride?'

'I'm afraid I'd have waited for ever for that. Marco must have somebody, or he'll end his days alone, and that would be terrible.'

'There are worse things than being alone, Aunt.'

'No, my dear boy, there aren't.'

He couldn't answer. For the first time in his life he felt it was true.

'I think you're just discovering that, aren't you?' she urged gently.

He shrugged. 'It's just a mood. I was away too long. Now I'm back there's a mountain of work to do....' His voice ran down.

'What is she like?'

He told his story again, this time taking longer to describe Selena. For once the words came easily to him and he managed to speak of the sweetness beneath the thorny shell, the way he'd discovered it slowly, and how it had captivated him.

'You love her very much, don't you?' Lucia said.

'No, I don't think I exactly—' he hastened to defend himself. 'It's just that I can't help worrying about her. She has nobody to look after her. She never has had anybody. Just people making use of her. The only family she has is Elliot. That's why it's breaking her heart knowing that his useful days are over. Apart from him, she's alone.'

'According to you she has quite a left hook.'

'Oh, she can take care of herself that way. But she's alone inside. I don't think I've ever met anyone as completely alone. She thinks she doesn't mind. She thinks she's happier that way.'

'Maybe she is. You've just said there are worse things.'

'I was wrong. When I think of her going on like that for years—fooling herself that she's happy, just getting more isolated—'

'It probably won't happen. She'll meet some nice young man and marry him. In a few years you'll bump into her again and she'll have a couple of children and another on the way.'

Leo grinned. 'You're a clever woman, Aunt. You know I don't want that.'

'I wonder what you do really want.'

'Whatever it is, I don't think I'll get it.'

The lights were going out along the Grand Canal. Behind them the great palace was closing down for the night. Leo rose and helped Lucia to her feet.

'Thank you for listening,' he said. 'I'm afraid Dulcie and Harriet thought me a bit of a clown.'

'Well, your life has been rather full of brief entanglements,' Lucia said, patting his hand. 'But if Selena is the right woman, you'll find her again. Although I think she's quite mad if *she* doesn't come to find *you*.'

'Maybe she doesn't want to find me,' Leo said gloomily. 'And even if she did, what good would it do me? She doesn't care for an ordinary life, in one place with a husband and kids.'

'I didn't know your thoughts had got that far.'

'They haven't,' he said quickly. 'I was talking generally.'

'Oh, I see.'

'She likes the open road, moving from place to place, never knowing what tomorrow may bring. So I probably couldn't make her happy anyway.'

'Enough of that kind of talk. If your love is fated to be, it will be. Now, tomorrow's a wedding. We're all going to enjoy ourselves.'

It was late when Selena came to a halt in the yard of the Four-Ten. Barton was waiting for her.

'Heard you really did well in Reno.'

'I'll be a millionaire yet,' she said. 'Barton, is something wrong?'

'I've heard from Leo.'

'Oh, really?'

'Don't you pretend you don't care. My guess is you're in as big a state as he is.'

'Why should he be in a state?'

'Because he lost your phone number. He's been going crazy, calling here, leaving messages for you to call him back.'

'But I didn't know—'

'No, I had to be away for a while, so I left word that if you called you were to be told all about it. Unfortunately the person I left word with was Paulie. Now, I don't know if he's just plum forgetful, or if there's more to it—' he looked at her face. 'Would this have anything to do with that time Paulie "stepped on a pitchfork"?'

'Well, I didn't want to tell you, when you've been so good to me—'

'If it helps any I've often wanted to sock him myself.'

'He just got a bit fresh, and I—well—'

'It was you? Not Leo?'

'In a pig's ear it was Leo. He came in when the fighting was over. But maybe I went too far.'

'Shouldn't think you did,' Barton said with relish. 'But you were quite right not to tell his mother. She overreacts to that kind of thing. Well, well, so he got his revenge.'

'Maybe I should call Leo now,' but Selena sounded vague and abstracted.

'Don't you want to?'

'Course I want to, but he's so far away, and he'll be another person in his own country.'

'Then go and find him in his own country. Find out if it can be your country. Selena, when a man keeps calling and getting agitated like this one has, then he has things to say to a woman that he can't say over the phone.'

'You mean me—go to Italy?'

'It's not the other side of the moon. You know I'll look after Jeepers and Elliot for you while you're gone. You've got all that prize money. What's stopping you?'

When she still didn't answer Barton began to cluck like a chicken.

'I am *not a chicken*.'

'Not when you're in the ring, sure. Never seen anyone braver. But that's the easy part. The world's a much scarier place. Maybe you should think about that.'

By the time he was on his way back home Leo had half talked himself into thinking things were for the best. This was fate's way of telling him that he and Selena weren't meant to be together.

The wedding had been a strain. The sight of his brother so blissfully happy as he'd become Dulcie's husband had made him suddenly discontented with his own lot.

Not that he was thinking of marriage for himself. The mere thought of Selena in the glimmering white satin and lace creation that Dulcie had worn put the whole matter into perspective. Selena would probably marry in a stetson and cowboy boots.

By the time he reached his own house he'd settled the matter in his mind. They'd had a great time together, but it was over, and that was as it should be. He wouldn't think of her any more.

Gina had just finished making up his bed. She greeted him and went to collect a duster that she'd left by the window.

'Renzo wanted to see you this afternoon,' she started to say, 'so that he can—I wonder who that is.'

'Who?' He went to stand beside her at the window that looked down on the path that led up from Morenza.

A tall slender figure, in jeans and shirt, and weighed down by a couple of bags, was walking towards the house, sometimes stopping to stare upward, her hand shading her eyes. She was too far away for Leo to see her face, but he recognised everything else, from her swaying walk to the angle of her head as she tilted it back.

'She must be a stranger in these parts,' Gina was saying, 'Because—*signore*?'

Her employer was no longer with her. She heard his feet thundering down the stairs and the next moment he appeared below, running so fast that Gina thought he would topple headlong into the valley.

The young woman dropped her bags and began to run too, and the next moment they were locked in each other's arms, oblivious to the rest of the world.

'Celia,' Gina yelled to one of the maids, 'We've got a guest. Stop what you're doing and prepare a room for her.

'Not,' she added, her eyes on the entwined figures, 'that I think she'll spend much time sleeping in it.'

CHAPTER EIGHT

'TELL me I'm not dreaming. You're really here!'

'I'm here, I'm here! Feel me.' Selena was laughing and crying together.

He did his best, crushing her in a fierce grip and kissing every part of her face.

'I've imagined you walking up that road so often but it was always a trick of the light.'

'Not this time. Oh, Leo, are you really glad to see me?'

Suddenly the words failed him. Was he glad to see her? All he knew was that the lump in his throat made it hard to speak.

'You're crying,' she said in wonder.

'Of course I'm not. Only wimps cry,' he teased her with the reminder of her own words. But his eyes were wet and he didn't dry them. He was a Latin, raised not to be ashamed of his emotions, and he had no wish to hide them with this woman.

164

He took her face between his hands, looking at her tenderly before laying his lips on hers in a long kiss. She answered, putting her heart into it, knowing this was why she'd come such a great distance, and nothing could have kept her away.

Something butted her from behind, then from the side, and she looked down to find herself surrounded by goats. They were coming down the hill, milling around the two of them, while a grinning goatherd made a gesture that was half greeting, half salute.

''*Notte* Franco,' Leo said, grinning back.

It would be all over the valley now, he thought. So let them talk!

He tucked one of Selena's bags under his arm, took the other in his hand, disentangled himself and her from curious goats, and put his free arm around her. Then, together they went up the hill to home.

'Are your family visiting you?' Selena asked, seeing all the faces at the windows.

'No, they're—' he stopped himself from saying '—the servants.' 'Two of the girls are Gina's nieces,' he said. It was true. When he needed to employ somebody new he just told

Gina and she produced some of her own vast family.

The faces vanished, and when they reached the door there was only Gina, smiling a welcome and explaining that the *signorina's* room was being prepared, and in the meantime refreshments were on their way from the kitchen.

Gina departed, and Leo took Selena back into his arms, not kissing her this time but pulling her against him and resting his head against her hair.

'How come she's already preparing a room for me?' Selena asked.

'She saw you come up the hill, and when I—when we—well, I guess everyone knows all about us by now.'

It was on the tip of her tongue to ask what he thought 'all about us' might be, but she let it go. She didn't know the answer herself. It was what she was here to find out. For the moment nothing mattered next to the joyous glow that enveloped her at being with him. In this country where everything looked strange and she didn't know the language she felt that she'd come home. Because he was here.

'Why didn't you take a cab all the way to the door?' Leo asked.

'I didn't know how to tell him your address. I found a bus which had 'Morenza' written on the front, only I didn't know you had to buy the tickets in a sweet shop first, and by the time I'd done that the bus had gone. Yes, all right, make fun of me.'

He was chuckling at her droll manner, but he controlled himself. 'I'm sorry, *carissima*, I can't help it. It was the way you said it. We are a little mad in Italy. We buy bus tickets in sweet shops.'

'What happens if the sweet shops are closed?'

'We walk.'

She gave a choke of laughter. He dropped his head so that his forehead rested against hers, and grinned with sheer delight at having her here.

'So I waited for the next bus,' she said, 'and then I recognised your house from what you'd told me.'

'But why didn't you call me to collect you?'

'Well—you know—'

All the way over she'd been tormented by the thought that he didn't really want her at all. She would call and hear the awkwardness in his voice. Perhaps he'd only called her in Texas to tell her not to call him because it had all been a big mistake. Only the fact that she was high above the Atlantic at the time stopped her getting out of the aircraft there and then.

She'd promised herself that when she landed she'd go straight back. Or call him. Or do anything rather than seek him out. Then she would hear again the sound of Barton clucking, and make herself go on, telling herself that no member of the Gates family had ever been a quitter. She had no idea if this were true, but it helped.

The bus had deposited her by the duck pond in Morenza, from where she could see the house at the top of the incline. There was an ancient cab waiting, and she could have simply pointed out the house to the driver, but she couldn't bring herself to do it—not if she might be coming back that way soon, a reject.

So she'd walked the last mile, dropping with weariness until a familiar and inexpressibly dear figure had come flying down to meet her, weeping with joy as he enfolded her against his heart. Then she'd known all she needed to know.

He showed her up to the room the maids had just finished, and on the way she looked at the house with its heavy stone walls. It was just as he'd told her, except for being much larger.

Her room, too, was large, with a polished wooden floor and the biggest bed she had ever seen, with a carved walnut head. The windows were guarded by heavy wooden shutters to keep out the heat, and when Gina pulled them open Selena could step out onto a tiny balcony to look down over the valley and the most beautiful countryside she had ever seen. The hills rolled away, greens and blues fading into misty distance, the lines broken by pine trees.

It was still warm enough to have supper outside, watching the sun set. Gina served them fish soup, a mixture of squid, prawns and mussels, garlic, onions and tomatoes. Selena felt that she'd died and gone to heaven.

'I got back to find Barton jumping up and down,' she said, sipping white wine. 'He'd left the message with Paulie who'd ''forgotten'' it.'

'But my irresistible attraction drew you anyway?' he ventured.

'I came to see the Grosseto rodeo,' she said firmly. 'That was all.'

'Nothing to do with me?'

'Nothing to do with you. Don't flatter yourself.'

'No, ma'am.'

'And you can stop grinning like that.'

'I wasn't grinning.'

'You were, like the cat that swallowed the cream. Just because I came halfway around the world looking for you, it doesn't mean anything. Do you understand that?'

'Sure. And just because I've spent the last few weeks going crazy looking through websites trying to get one step ahead of you, that doesn't mean anything either.'

'Fine!'

'Fine!'

They sat in silence, contemplating each other with joy.

'You did it again,' she said. 'When I arrived you called me *carissima*, but you didn't tell me what it meant.'

'In Italian *cara* means dear,' he said. 'And when you add *issima* it's a kind of emphasis, the most extreme form of something that you can say.'

She was looking at him.

'And so you see,' he said, taking her hand, 'when a man calls a woman *carissima*—'

Suddenly it was hard. In the past he'd used the word casually, almost without meaning. Now everything was different and he was left only with the old debased currency.

'It means that she is more than dear to him,' he said. 'It means—'

He broke off as Gina returned for the plates. '*Tagliatelle* with pumpkin, *signore*,' she said.

Smiling, Leo let it go. There would be time later to say everything he wanted to say.

They finished the meal with Tuscan honey and nut cake. By then Selena's eyes were closing. At last Leo took her hand and led her upstairs, stopping at her door.

'Goodnight,' he said softly. '*Carissima.*'

'Goodnight.'

He kissed her cheek and left her.

He lay awake most of that night. The knowledge that she was sleeping next door made him feel like a man with hoarded treasure under his roof. The treasure was his and he would keep it, fighting off the world if need be.

He awoke in the early dawn and went to the window, opening the shutters and standing out on the small balcony. He was still filled with a sense of wonder at her coming, and he wanted to look again at the road that led down to the village, a road he'd so often gazed at, longing to see her, until one day she'd been there.

A shadow in the next window made him look. She was standing there, not looking at him but down into the valley, her face quiet and absorbed, as though in another world.

As he watched, she raised her head long enough to give him a brief smile, but then became absorbed once more in watching the valley.

Now he understood.

Throwing on a robe he slipped out of his own room and into hers, coming up behind her at the window and laying his hands gently on her shoulders. When she leaned back on him he slid his arms around her so that they crossed over her chest. She raised her hands to curve over his forearms, and he held her there against him, filled with a deep contentment that was unlike anything he'd ever known in his life before.

Down below them a soft glow was creeping over the valley, faint at first, then growing in intensity. The light was magical, unearthly, for just a few blessed moments.

Then it changed, grew harsher, firmer, more prosaic, ready for the working day. Only the memory was left.

Selena gave a little sigh of satisfaction, so quiet that he sensed it through his flesh rather than heard it.

'That's what I wanted,' she said. 'Ever since you told me about that light, I've longed to see it.'

'What did you think?'

'It was just as beautiful as you promised. The most beautiful thing I ever saw.'

'It'll be there again tomorrow,' he said. 'But now—'

He drew her gently back into the room and took her to bed, where they found another kind of beauty.

In his mind Leo had often imagined the moment when he introduced Selena to Peri, the mare who had been ready for him to sell for months, but whose elegance and spirit had made him keep her back, waiting for the right person.

Selena was that person. He'd always suspected it and he knew for sure when he witnessed their love at first sight. By now he reckoned he knew a bit about love at first sight.

He thought perhaps he would give Peri to her as a wedding present. He no longer shied away from that kind of thought. A man should know how to accept when it was all up with him.

They spent their days riding his fields and vineyards, and their nights in each other's arms.

'Stay here,' he said one night when they had loved each other to exhaustion. 'Don't leave me again.'

She made the little restless movement that he always sensed at any mention of permanency, and he quickly added, 'Take charge of the horses. Take charge of me. Either or both, as you like.'

She raised herself on one elbow and looked down into his face. The shutters were open, flooding the room with moonlight, throwing shadows between her breasts, absorbing all his attention so that he didn't hear her question.

'What was that?' he murmured, tracing the swell with his finger.

'I said it was about time you finished telling me what *carissima* means.'

As she spoke she was easing herself over him, moving slowly and with purpose.

'If you are my *carissima*,' he said, 'you are dearer to me than all the world. You are my love, my beloved, the only one who exists for me.'

A week later they went to Maremma, an area in the south of Tuscany, near the coast. It was often known as 'the Wild West of Tuscany', since there cattle were raised in large numbers, and the traditional cowboy skills were still in everyday use.

Each year this was celebrated by a rodeo that consisted of a parade through the nearby town of Grosseto, and a show that lasted one afternoon. Leo took Selena to the town to meet the organisers, describing her achievements in glowing terms.

Then Selena produced a surprise of her own. All the way over she'd been clutching a large, flat object, refusing to let Leo see it. It turned out to be a photograph of him bull riding.

'I know this guy who takes photographs of everything,' she said, 'even the people who don't win. I looked him up, and he had this one of you. You look real good, don't you?'

He looked magnificent. One arm was high in the air, his head was up, his face full of a wide grin of delight and triumph.

'You'd never know that I was off the next second,' he said.

One of the organisers regarded the picture and coughed respectfully.

'Perhaps, *signore*, you could give us a demonstration of bull riding, at our rodeo.'

'I don't think so,' Leo said hastily. 'They have very special bulls in Texas. Bred for their ferocity.'

'I don't think we would disappoint you, *signore*. We have a bull here that has already gored two men to death—'

It took Leo ten minutes to talk his way out of that one, with Selena doubled up with laughter.

'I told him that you'd demonstrate barrel racing,' he told her as they made their escape.

'That's fine. But it won't be the same without you riding that bull.'

'Get lost!'

Leo's family had never made the trip before. This year, however, they were coming in force, for by now they knew what everyone knew— that Leo, the all-embracing lover of ladies with voluptuous forms, had fallen 'victim' to an angular young woman with a figure like a rail and a head like fire. Temper, ditto.

So the bulk of the Calvani family planned to head for the farm to stay the night before going on to Grosseto. Only Marco was missing. The Count and Countess Calvani, with Guido and Dulcie, would be travelling from Venice.

Knowing these plans were afoot, Leo knew that the day of reckoning couldn't be postponed much longer. Some time soon he must confess all to Selena—his reprehensible wealth or his shocking connection to a title. It was a moot point which one would horrify her the most.

While he was still trying to broach the subject he was overtaken by events. Selena, seeking him one morning, came to his study.

'Leo, are you in here?'

She pushed the door further open. There was no sign of Leo but she could hear his voice coming from the passage beyond, and went further into the room to wait for him.

Then something caught her eye.

Several photographs were spread out on the desk, and curiosity drew her over to look at them. What she saw made her first frown, then stare.

They were wedding pictures, reminding her that Leo had recently been to the marriage of his brother, Guido. There were the bride and groom, the bride gorgeous in white satin and lace, the groom with a wicked, appealing face. And there, next to him, was Leo, dressed as she'd never seen him before.

Dressed for best. In costly finery. With a top hat!

So what? Everyone dressed up at weddings.

But there was something in the background that wouldn't be dismissed. Chandeliers, old pictures, mirrors with gilt frames. The clothes fitted perfectly, which hired clothes never did. And the people had the awesome confidence that came with money and status.

A strange feeling, something like dismay, was starting to take over her stomach, prior to invading the rest of her.

'They just arrived.'

Leo was standing in the doorway, smiling in the way that could make her forget everything else.

'Let me introduce you to my family,' he said, coming forward and sorting the pictures. 'That's my brother Guido, and Dulcie. These two cheesy characters here are her father and brother, and if I never see them again it'll be too soon. This one here is my cousin Marco, and that's his fiancée Harriet. And this man is my uncle Francesco, and his wife, Liza.'

'What's that place behind all of you. Did you hire the town hall or something?'

'No,' he said casually, 'that's my uncle's home.'

'That? He lives there? It's like a palace.'

Leo's tone became even more casual. 'I suppose that's what it is, really.'

'What do you mean?'

'It's called the Palazzo Calvani. It's on the Grand Canal in Venice.'

'Your uncle lives in a palace? What is he, royalty?'

'No, no, nothing so grand. Just a count.'

'What was that? You mumbled that last word.'

'He's a count,' Leo said reluctantly.

She stared at him. 'You're related to a real count?'

'Yes, but on the wrong side of the blanket,' he assured her, like a man arguing mitigating circumstances to a crime.

'But they know you, don't they?' she accused him. 'You're part of the family.'

He sighed and admitted it.

'My father was Uncle Francesco's brother. If his marriage to my mother had been valid I'd be—well—the heir.'

She turned an appalled gaze on him.

'But it wasn't,' he placated her, 'so I'm not. That's Guido's problem, not mine. And boy is he mad at me about it. Like it was my fault. He doesn't want it any more than I do. All I ever wanted was this farm and the life I have here. You've got to believe me, Selena.'

'Give me one reason I should ever believe a word you say again.'

'Now, come on, I never lied to you.'

'You sure as heck never told me the truth either.'

'Well, did you give me your life story from day one?'

'*Yes.*'

She had him there.

'And you're not being logical,' he changed tack hastily. 'If I was that poor, how come I knew Barton, and went to visit him?'

'You sold him some horses, you told me. And you can get cheap air tickets these days. And there's other things. This place, the people, the land—the way you talked I thought

you rented some dirt-poor little place at the
back of beyond, but you own it don't you?'

'I've never pretended about that.'

'And how much do you own? You're the
padrone, aren't you? Not just here but the village and halfway to Florence, for all I know.'

'Rather more than that, actually,' he confessed miserably.

'You could buy Barton out, couldn't you?'

He shrugged. 'I don't know. Probably.'

'I thought you were just a country boy—you
let me think that. But you're really more like
a—a tycoon.'

'I *am* a country boy.'

'You're a country tycoon, that's what you
are.'

She was pale with shock.

'Leo, be honest with me for the first time
since we've known each other. Just how rich
are you?'

'Darn it, Selena, are you only going to
marry me for my money?'

'I'm not going to marry you at all, you con-
ceited—'

'I didn't mean it like that, you know I
didn't.'

'All those things I said to you, about millionaires not being real people—'

'Well, now you know you were wrong.'

'The hell I do! I reckon you've proved me right about all the worst. I wouldn't have thought you could do a thing like this to me!'

'What have I done?' he implored the room. 'Will someone please tell me what I've done?'

'You've pretended to be one thing, while actually being another.'

'Well, of course I did,' he roared. 'I wasn't going to take the chance on losing you. Think I didn't know? Sure I knew. We hadn't met five minutes before I knew you were the most awkward, unreasonable female with no common sense. I didn't want to scare you off, so we played by your rules. I couldn't even tell you I'd—' He stopped with his feet at the edge of the precipice.

'Tell me you'd done what?'

'I forget.' But then, with her eyes on him he reckoned he might as well be hung for a sheep as a lamb. 'All right, the van and the horse trailer—they came from me.'

'You—bought the replacement van—and horse trailer?'

'And Jeepers. Selena, the insurers would have laughed at you. You knew that yourself. It was the only way to get you back on the road. I just hoped you wouldn't find out, or that you wouldn't be too mad at me if you did.' He studied her face, hardly daring to believe what he saw there. 'Why—are you laughing?'

'You mean—' she choked '—that you were the miracle after all? Not Barton?'

'Yes, me, not Barton.'

'No wonder you looked green around the gills when I said that.'

'I could have killed him,' Leo confessed. 'I wanted to tell you the truth but I couldn't, because I knew you wouldn't want to be beholden to me. But I've thought of a way around that. We get married and then it's your wedding present, and we're all straight.'

She stared. 'You're serious, aren't you?'

'Well, the way I see it, if you marry me, all that disgusting money will be yours too, and then you'll have to shut up about it.'

She considered this. 'OK, it's a deal.'

She didn't say she loved him then. She said it later that night, when he was breathing deeply beside her, the sleep of peace and satiety, as he always did when they'd released each other from passion by indulging it without limit. He slept heavily, so she could smooth his hair, kiss him without his knowing, and whisper the words she didn't know how to say when he heard her.

Another night he brought wine and peaches, and they sat feasting and talking.

'How do your family come to be out here?' she asked. 'If you're Venetian counts, what are you doing in Tuscany?'

'How can you ask? Everyone knows the evil aristos commandeer property wherever they can. That's how we keep our feet on the necks of the deserving poor.'

'Oh, very funny! I'll thump you in a minute. What are you doing here?'

'My grandfather, Count Angelo, fell in love with a woman from Tuscany, called Maria Rinucci. This—' he indicated the valley '—was her dowry. Since he had the Venetian property to bequeath to his eldest son and heir—that's my uncle Francesco—this was used to provide an inheritance for Francesco's younger brothers, Bertrando and Silvio.

'Silvio took his share in cash and married a banker's daughter in Rome. Their son is Marco. You won't meet him next week because something's gone wrong between him and Harriet, his English fiancée. She's gone back to England and he's followed her, trying to talk her around. Let's hope he brings her back for our wedding.'

He stroked her face, trying to distract her with the thought of their wedding. She accepted his caress and kissed him enthusiastically, but she wouldn't be distracted.

'And?' she insisted.

'Bertrando liked living on the land, so he came out here and married a widow, Elissa, who became my mother.

'She died soon after I was born, and he married again, Donna, Guido's mother. But then it turned out that Elissa hadn't been a widow, as everyone had thought, but still married to her first husband. So I was illegitimate, and as she was dead it was too late to validate her marriage to my father, so that was that. Guido and I kind of swapped inheritances.

'I can't tell you how glad I am now that we did. Because otherwise, you and I—'

'Nix,' she said as he'd known she would say. 'I couldn't marry you if you had a title. It's against my principles, and besides—well anyway, it doesn't matter. But your family wouldn't fancy me as the countess.'

'You don't know anything about them. Forget those stereotypes you're carrying in your head. We don't all eat off gold plate—'

'Shame, I was looking forward to that.'

'Will you hush, and let me finish? And don't look at me like that or I'll forget what I was going to stay.'

'Well, there are more interesting things to do—'

'When I've finished,' he said, seizing her wandering fingers. 'My family aren't the way you think. All they'll care about is that we love each other. Guido and Dulcie have just married for love, so did Uncle Francesco. He waited forty years for her to say yes, and refused to marry anyone else. She had some funny ideas too and he was a patient man, but I'm not. If you think I'm waiting forty years for you to see sense, you're nuts. Now, you were saying about doing more interesting things...'

CHAPTER NINE

SELENA had tried to keep it light, but she was more nervous about Leo's family than she would have let on. He'd said her head was full of stereotypes, and it was partly true. Her dread was concentrated on the thought of doing or saying something that would embarrass Leo by drawing down icy stares on herself. She would rather ride a bull than risk looking foolish.

With a few days to go the house was turned upside down. Leo and Selena changed rooms, retreating to smaller ones at the back of the house so that his uncle and aunt might have the best, with Guido and Dulcie in the next best.

It made Selena stare to see Gina preparing the house for a gala occasion, with the assistance of two maids, a cook and two extra girls in from the village. Being waited on by servants unnerved her.

'Well, you're the mistress of the house now,' Leo said. 'Dismiss the lot of them, and do it virtuously yourself.'

'Oh, yeah?' she demanded, checkmated. Leo's eyes were full of wicked fun.

'You could do all the cooking as well,' he suggested.

'Have you tasted my cooking?'

'Have I—? I had a sandwich you made the other day, and I'm still getting up in the night. Leave them to their job, *carissima*, and you get on with your job, which is the horses.'

She was virtually running that side of things now. Things were simpler with horses. You knew what was expected of you. That made her think of Elliot, and she felt a pang of homesickness. Elliot was the faithful friend who'd seen her through the bad times, and whom she might never see again.

After the first bout of homesickness she found it could attack again without warning. The sheer grandeur of the house when Gina had finished transforming it had the same effect on her, making her think of a mini van, a battered horse trailer at the back, Elliot and herself chasing the far horizons with just enough money to reach the next stop, then relying on each other to win some for the next stage.

There were far horizons here, she thought, looking out on Tuscany's rolling hills, but they seemed somehow tame now that she knew they belonged to Leo, and by extension to herself. There was no mystery in a horizon that you owned. And no excitement either.

But she pushed those thoughts aside. She knew the coming visit was important to Leo. Whatever he might say to disparage his aristocratic background, these people were the family he loved, and she suspected that he shared their values more than he realised. The thought made him seem a little distant.

As the day grew nearer she became so demoralised that when Leo suggested that she buy a couple of dresses she made no protest. She chose items as unobtrusive as possible because she was no longer sure of herself, and she didn't want to be noticed.

Count Francesco Calvani had decided to travel the hundred and sixty miles from Venice in his own chauffeur-driven limousine, which he felt would be more comfortable for his beloved Liza, who disliked trains.

Guido and Dulcie travelled in their own jaunty sports car. With a stop at Florence for lunch they made Bella Podena by late afternoon. They had driven ahead of the two, and arrived before them.

'We just couldn't wait to meet you,' Guido said, enveloping Selena in a hug.

She liked him at once. He bore very little physical resemblance to his brother, but their eyes had the same twinkle. In Leo perhaps it was warmer, and in Guido more mischievous, but it was the link between them.

Dulcie was almost as slender as Selena herself, but with a mass of wavy blonde hair that Selena secretly envied. She too hugged her, and said eagerly how glad she was that she would soon have a sister. Selena began to relax.

A few minutes later they gathered outside for the arrival of the Count and Countess Calvani. The shiny black car glided to a standstill, the chauffeur emerged and proceeded to open one of the passenger doors.

From it descended a tiny woman with a lean face and hooded eyes. Selena had a strange feeling that she was full of tension as she looked around her.

I'll bet she's looking down on us because this is a farm, she thought, angry for Leo's sake. Just because she's used to a palace…

She saw the count appear from his side of the car and smile at his wife, who smiled back and laid her hand on his arm. Together they entered the house, and the introductions were made.

Count Francesco Calvani had the family charm. He too embraced Selena like a long-lost daughter and spoke to her in excellent English. Liza smiled and shook her hand, then made a stilted little speech of welcome which had to be translated into English. Selena thanked her in terms equally stilted, which the count translated into Venetian.

The two women looked at each other across a chasm.

As mistress of the house Selena escorted Liza to her room, and gave thanks for Dulcie who came too, and translated them to each other. She finally escaped, thanking heaven for a merciful release, and had a horrible feeling that the countess was doing the same.

She had a feeling of being stranded in a desert. She'd spent the last few years doing something she did well, and because of it she had confidence in herself. But now her confidence seemed to have drained away through the soles of her feet. Everything she did felt wrong, even when Leo smiled encouragement and told her she was doing well.

Her dress felt dowdy beside the countess's quiet elegance and Dulcie's glowing beauty. When Gina drew her into the dining room to approve the elegant table settings she wanted to sink from the conviction that Gina knew that refined dining was a mystery to her, and despised her accordingly.

'That's great,' she said desperately. 'It looks lovely, Gina.'

'The food is ready to serve, *signorina*.'

'In that case—I suppose I should bring people in.'

She did this by conveying the message to Leo and letting him make the announcement. She knew she should have done it herself, but she would rather have ridden a bull than stand up in that company and invite them into 'her' dining room. She began to wonder when there was a flight back to Texas.

Things improved a little when she found herself talking to Dulcie. They swapped stories about 'life before Calvani' as Dulcie teasingly put it. Dulcie was thrilled by Selena's background.

'I've always loved Westerns,' she said longingly. 'You mean you do real Wild West stuff? Roping and riding and such?'

'Riding. I don't actually do roping—although, I can. This guy showed me how. Said I was pretty good.'

'Are you going to do roping at Grosseto tomorrow?'

Selena shook her head. 'Women don't do that in rodeos. We just do barrel racing.'

Dulcie's eyes were mischievous. 'Do you think the Grosseto organisers know that?'

Selena grinned. 'You're wicked,' she said appreciatively, and Dulcie nodded.

From the other end of the table Guido and Leo watched their womenfolk with satisfaction.

'We always do it,' Guido observed.

'What's that?' his brother asked.

'Uncle Francesco has a saying that the Calvanis always choose the best, the best food, the best wine, the best women. We did well, brother. Both of us.'

The meal was superb. The count congratulated Leo's cook and the atmosphere became genial. This lasted until the subject of the wedding came up, and the count immediately declared that of course it must take place in St Mark's Basilica, in Venice.

'Selena and I thought the parish church in Morenza would suit us,' Leo said.

'The parish—?' The count seemed lost for words. 'A Calvani, marry in a village?'

'This is our home,' Leo said firmly. 'It's what Selena and I both wish.'

'But—'

'No, uncle,' Leo said firmly.

He would have said more but the countess laid her hand on his arm and said something Selena didn't understand, except that she caught her own name.

'All right, all right,' he said placatingly. 'I won't say any more.'

He patted his wife's hand and responded in the same language she'd used.

You didn't have to be a genius to know what they'd said, Selena reckoned. The countess couldn't think what the fuss was about. St Mark's was too good for Selena Gates. And the count had agreed with her.

Luckily everyone wanted an early night, to be ready for the pleasures of the following day. Normally Selena slept easily, but tonight she lay awake for hours, wondering what she was doing here.

They left early for Grosseto, the family to take up position in a hotel room Leo had booked for them, which overlooked the procession. Leo and Selena went straight to the meeting place from where the procession was to start.

Today they were both dressed to kill, in the finest available from Delia's stall, cowboy shirts, buttoned to the neck, colourful cowboy boots and belts with large silver buckles. When Leo had rammed a stetson squarely on his head, and Selena had settled hers on at a rakish angle they were ready for the parade.

It was quite a parade. The town band had turned out in force, well rehearsed, and if it sounded a little too Italian to be authentic nobody cared for that. The horsemen, or *butteri* as they were known locally, had the rough splendour of men who lived hard lives and performed the difficult feats of roping and riding not only in performance but in their everyday lives.

After the parade everyone moved to a nearby field for the contests that would take up the afternoon. First off was the bucking-bronco contest. Leo had elected to enter this, and did creditably without winning. Then the barrels were set up, a voice from a loudspeaker told the crowd all about Selena and predicted that she would do the circuit in no more than fourteen seconds.

This gave her a real challenge as the barrels were set just too far apart for that, and Peri lacked experience. The two of them gave it all they had, taking fourteen and a half, which didn't stop the announcer yelling, 'Fourteen seconds,' as she finished. And the cheerful crowd took his word for it.

If she thought the day was over she had a shock coming. Next came the calf roping, and some mischievous person had entered her in it. Guido always swore that it wasn't him.

Like Leo she managed well enough not to lose face, and the afternoon ended in a riot of good fellowship. The Calvanis cheered her to the echo, all except the countess, who applauded, but quietly, and left Selena wondering what she was really thinking. 'Brash and unladylike, I reckon,' she thought. 'Can't be helped.'

There were a dozen food stalls selling local specialities, and they all consumed freely, even the countess, who tucked in with gusto.

'She comes from these parts,' Leo explained. 'She doesn't often get the chance of good Tuscan eats.'

But by the time they reached home everyone was hungry again, and Selena's thoughts had flown back across the Atlantic.

'I could just do with a hot dog,' she sighed.

'We could make some,' Gina said. 'What do we need?'

'Sausages and rolls.'

'Rolls we have. Sausages I must send for.'

'But it's late, the shops are shut.'

'I will send Sara. The butcher is her uncle.'

In half an hour the little maid was back with her uncle's finest. Selena made hot dogs, Tuscan style, and everybody pronounced them excellent.

Even the countess ate two, Selena noticed. And she smiled at her, and said, *'Grazie, Selena.'*

Afterwards, as they drank coffee and sipped wine, Dulcie said to her, 'Do you know, you're just the way I expected.'

Selena was startled. 'You knew about me?'

'When Leo came back from Texas he couldn't talk about anything else but you, how he'd met you, and you were wonderful, and he didn't have your number any more. He was going crazy. If you hadn't come over here, I'm pretty sure he'd have taken off to find you.'

Selena looked up to find Leo's eyes on them. He was grinning, embarrassed, but too good-natured to mind being laughed at.

'So now you know,' he told Selena.

'Go on,' she ribbed him, 'I knew anyway. Always reckoned you couldn't resist me.'

He slipped a friendly arm about her.

'On the other hand,' he mused, 'It was you who came looking for me.'

'In a pig's eye I came looking for you. I came for the rodeo.'

'Sure you did.'

'Sure I did.'

'Well, it's over now,' he said, 'so you can go back.' But his arm tightened as he spoke.

The others were watching them, smiling.

'Then I'll go,' she said defiantly.

'Fine. Go.' The arm tightened.

'I'm going.'

'Good.'

'Good.'

'Oh, get on with it and kiss each other,' Guido said in exasperation. 'I need a drink. Ouch!' He rubbed his ribs which had collided with a wifely elbow.

After that everybody sat up much too late, unwilling to let a happy occasion end. Toast followed toast until they all trooped off to bed.

Next morning they parted with many promises to see each other soon, when Leo and Selena tied the knot. Even the countess smiled and kissed Selena's cheek, so that she began to feel she'd been worrying about nothing.

She and Leo stood, arms entwined, until the last car had vanished from sight. Then they hurried back to work.

Now they were in the season of harvests. Leo had grapes and olives to bring safely in, and there would be no time to marry until that was done. Selena became fascinated by this side of their lives, and spent long hours in the saddle, riding his acres with him.

They would return every evening, worn out but content, and satisfied with what they were bringing to fruition. Gradually her restlessness abated. There was nothing to worry about, and this happy life would go on forever.

The phone call came out of the blue one morning. Selena emerged from the shower to find Leo looking harassed.

'Uncle Francesco has been on the telephone. He wants us to drop everything and go to Venice now, this minute.'

'Is he crazy. We're about to start bringing in the grapes.'

'That's what I told him. He just said it was urgent.'

'You don't think he wants to have another go at you about the wedding.'

'I hope it's not that. I've told him time and again we're going to marry in Morenza and that's final. If he's dragged us all the way to Venice to have the argument again, I'll—' he searched for something that his amiable temper could rise to '—I'll tell him he shouldn't have done it.'

'So you're going?'

'We're going. I must have a talk to Renzo and then I'll get the car out.' He groaned. 'Why couldn't he at least tell me what's happened? Ah well, the sooner we're there the sooner we'll know, and the sooner we can get home.'

As they neared the city Selena asked, 'If the streets of Venice are water, where do we park the car?'

'There's a causeway that stretches from the mainland, over the lagoon, to Venice. At the Venice end is a terminus called Piazzale Roma where we leave the car and take the boat the rest of the way.'

'A gondola?'

'No, they don't work like taxis. They just do round trips for tourists. Uncle will have sent his boat for us.'

But when they got there they were greeted by a surprise. It was Guido who greeted them, and the boat he'd brought with him was a gondola.

'I'd forgotten that you fancied yourself as a gondolier,' Leo said with a grin. To Selena he added, 'Guido has some gondolier friends, and he borrows their boat whenever the mood takes him. It's his idea of honest toil.'

'Ignore him,' Guido said, kissing Selena and assisting her into the gondola.

He put their bags in, then turned to usher Leo into the boat with a theatrical flourish. '*Signore!*'

'You're up to something, little brother,' Leo said with a grin.

'Who, me?'

'Don't give me that innocent look. You always looked innocent when you'd done something that made everyone groan. What do you know that I don't?'

'The things I know that you don't would fill a book,' Guido ribbed him. 'Don't blame me. It's life. Fate. Kismet.'

He cast off, and for a while Selena was distracted by her first gondola ride and her first visit to Venice. It seemed like no time before they had glided out of a side canal into the Grand Canal, the great highway through the centre of town.

'That's where Uncle lives,' Leo said, indicating a building on the right.

The Palazzo Calvani was a monumental building, whose front was decorated with stone decorations of a lacy appearance that almost disguised its size. Selena could understand why it was called a palace. It exuded confidence and beauty in equal measure. It had been the home of great lords for centuries, and its spirit bowed to no man.

She could appreciate the beauty and the confidence, while being profoundly glad that nobody was asking her to live in it.

The impression was heightened as they drew up to the landing stage and there were servants, reaching forward to help them. Then the big, glamorous house seemed to reach out too, enveloping them.

'I know,' Leo murmured in her ear. 'Sometimes I don't think I'm going to escape alive either.'

She chuckled and felt better. If they were together in this, it wasn't so bad.

Her eyes widened when she saw her room. Even the Four-Ten hadn't been as outrageous as this.

'It's as big as a tennis court,' she muttered to Leo. 'We'll get lost in it.'

'Not us, you,' he said. 'My room's at the other end of the corridor.'

'They haven't put us together? Why?'

'Because we're not married. We have to think of the proprieties.'

'But they know we're together.'

'I know we are, and they know we are. But we're not supposed to know that they know, and they're not supposed to know that we know they know. And none of us can admit what anyone knows. It's called doing things properly.'

'It's called sticking your head in the sand.'

'That too,' he agreed.

Then Selena saw something that made her jump.

'Leo, who's that, and what's she doing with my bag?'

'That Liza's maid,' Dulcie said, slipping in behind them 'She sent her to help you.'

'You mean she thinks I'm useless by my-self?'

'Stop being so prickly,' Dulcie said. 'It's meant as a compliment, because you're an honoured guest.'

You could take it like that, Selena reckoned. Or you could take it as a subtle insult, a way of saying the countess just knew you wouldn't have a maid of your own. That was the trouble with these folk. You didn't know which way to take them.

She'd counted on Leo for support, but she soon realised that he only half understood. Whatever he might say about not being at ease in this place, the fact remained that this was his family, and he loved them. They had shared history, and shared thoughts that needed no words. They called him 'the country bumpkin' in a tone of half-derisive affection, but he was one of them in a way Selena knew she never could be.

From then on she felt a double meaning in everything. When the countess came to her room and personally took her down to supper, was this a compliment, or a wordless way of saying she was too stupid to find the way? When the count rose to take her hand, murmur a compliment on her dress, and lead her to the table, wasn't he really noticing that the dress had been bought in the Morenza market?

Well, they weren't going to intimidate her.

She took a deep breath and accepted the seat of honour, at right angles to the count. After that she managed pretty well. Her fear was that she might mishandle one of the priceless crystal goblets, and smash it, but the light, skilful touch that had carried her through countless races came to her aid. It was like a horse, really. The trick was not to grab, but to caress.

The food was superb, and even her morbid sensitivity couldn't turn that into an insult. She was beginning to relax when there was a faint commotion from just outside the dining room. The next moment the Calvani family had risen *en masse* to welcome a man and a woman who had come into the room.

'Marco!' the count cried joyfully. 'Harriet!'

A tall, elegantly handsome man stood there with a statuesque young woman.

'I didn't dare to hope you could make it,' the count said, going forward eagerly to embrace the two of them.

'We just managed to get a flight,' Marco said. 'We weren't going to miss the big occasion if we could help it. Have you—?'

'No, no, not yet,' the count said hurriedly cutting him off. 'Come, both of you, and meet the newest member of our family.'

Selena's eyes met Leo's over the table, both equally puzzled. Big occasion?

So this was Marco, she thought, the cousin Leo had mentioned, the one who never showed his feelings but had gone chasing off to England, neglecting his banking job in Rome, in order to win back the woman he loved. Now his manner was cool and composed, as though such emotional behaviour was beyond him. Yet she noticed how his eyes constantly wandered to Harriet, as though he couldn't quite believe that she was there.

She'd taken an instant liking to Dulcie, and now she found herself liking Harriet who sat beside her and chattered between mouthfuls as she hurried to catch up with the meal.

'I'm so glad you and Leo managed to get it together,' she said. 'Dulcie and I hoped you would.'

'I've already told her how much he talked about her,' Dulcie said.

Harriet nodded. 'I remember that.'

'Actually the two of you thought me very funny,' Leo said, overhearing. He grinned at Harriet. 'But the laugh's on Marco now. You must really have gotten under his skin to make him follow you all the way to London, and stay there for weeks. When are you going to make an honest man of him?'

'Well, it'll have to be soon,' Harriet said, laughing. 'He's giving me the shop as a wedding present. I have an antique shop,' she said to Harriet. 'The trouble is I'm a terrible businesswoman, so Marco's been teaching me "financial common sense".'

'Antiques?' Selena said in a hollow voice. 'You mean—?' She looked at their surroundings, the crystal chandeliers, the priceless paintings. 'You mean—this kind of stuff?'

'Oh, yes,' Harriet said eagerly. 'This place makes my mouth water it's so full of history and beauty. You could sum up the story of Venice in this house, the people, the occasions—'

Selena didn't hear any more. A depression had settled over her heart. For one moment she'd hoped to find a kindred spirit in Harriet, someone who might also feel like a fish out of water in these surroundings. And now it turned out that she belonged here as much as any Calvani. She would fit seamlessly into the family, and underline the fact that Selena herself stuck out like a sore thumb.

Still, she thought, there was always Dulcie, the private detective, the working girl who'd known what it was to scrabble for a living.

She had to cling to that thought, because she was realising that there were thoughts she couldn't share with Leo. He simply didn't understand.

And that was the worst thing of all.

CHAPTER TEN

THE meal was drawing to a close. The plates had been cleared and there were coffee and liqueurs on the table. A hush fell on the conversation, as though everyone recognised that the time had come.

'Does everybody have a glass?' the count demanded. 'Splendid. Then I have an announcement to make.' His eyes fell on Leo and Selena.

Oh no! she thought. This is to tell us that he's arranged our marriage in St Marks, and we just have to fall into line.

'As you know,' Francesco went on, 'soon we will all be going to Tuscany for the marriage of our dear Leo and Selena. A joyful occasion, made even more joyful by what I have to tell you.'

A pause. He seemed uncertain how to go on. Selena relaxed. At least it wasn't the wedding.

'It's another wedding I wish to speak of tonight,' Francesco continued. 'One that we

211

thought—that is, we have been in some confusion all these years—but now that things are
clear—'

He looked at Guido. 'You tell them,' he
said. 'This is your story.'

Guido took the floor and addressed Leo.
'Uncle Francesco's trying to tell you that it
was a mistake about your mother's marriage
all those years ago. She never was married before. So her marriage to our father was valid,
and you're legitimate.'

In the thunderstruck silence Selena saw Leo
turn pale. Then he managed some kind of
laugh.

'Very funny, little brother. You were always
good for a joke, and that's your best yet.'

'It's no joke,' Guido said. 'It's all been
proved. That man who turned up alive, saying
Elissa was his wife—Franco Vinelli. They
were never married. Vinelli had been married
before, in England. He was an actor, in a
Commedia dell'Arte troop, and they toured all
over.

'He married an Englishwoman in a register
office. When his tour ended he just abandoned
her. He seems to have thought an English civil

ceremony wouldn't count when he got back to Italy.'

'He was right,' Leo said firmly. 'It wouldn't be recognised over here, not in those days.'

'But it was,' Guido said. 'There was an international convention, saying that if a marriage was valid in the country where it was contracted then it would be recognised in any other country that was a signatory. Both England and Italy were signatories, so the marriage counted here.

'He was a married man when he took Elissa to wife, which means that she was a free woman when she married our father. Their marriage was legitimate. And so are you.'

'What do you mean it's all been proved?' Leo demanded. 'What can be proved after all this time?'

'It can be done, with a little ferreting around.'

'Which I'll bet you did.'

'Sure. I never wanted all this, never pretended about it. It's all yours.'

Leo was looking around him with a trapped look.

'This is nonsense,' he said. 'You have to forget it.'

'It's the law,' the count roared. 'It cannot be forgotten. You are my heir, and that is how it should be. You've always been the eldest son—'

'The illegitimate eldest son,' Leo said firmly.

'Not any more,' Marco reminded him.

'You keep out of this,' Leo ordered him, 'You—you *banker*!'

Marco poured himself a drink, unperturbed.

'It's too late to change anything,' Leo insisted. 'I don't believe in this so-called proof. It wouldn't stand up to scrutiny by a lawyer—'

'It already has,' Guido said. 'It's been gone over and over by lawyers, sworn statements, properly notarised, records from the English registers.'

'What does Vinelli say?' Leo challenged. 'Bring him here to face me.'

'Vinelli died last year. He had no family, and nobody near him knew about that English marriage.'

'There must be somebody.'

'There's only written records.'

'I'll bet you thought of every detail,' Leo fumed.

'You bet I did.'

'You're loving this, aren't you?' Leo flung at him.

'Every minute.'

'That's fine for you but what about—' Leo's eyes fell on Selena, pale and distraught, watching him beseechingly. 'What about us?' he finished quietly, taking her hand.

She rose and stood beside him. The sight of them side by side seemed to alert the others to the fact that something was really wrong. This wasn't the joyous announcement that Count Francesco had counted on.

The count began to huff and puff. 'Well, I must say, I expected better than this,' he said. 'It should be a great day.'

'Having your life overturned doesn't make for a great day,' Leo said firmly. 'Now, if you'll excuse us, Selena and I will go upstairs. We've got some talking to do.'

They walked from the room, hand in hand, and broke into a run as soon as they were out of sight. They didn't stop until they reached his room.

'Leo, they can't do this to us.'

'Don't you worry, I won't let them.'

But she heard the uncertainty in his voice and it made her shiver. She'd always known him light-hearted in the face of any challenge, as though nothing could ever be too much for him. Now she sensed that he didn't feel confident of overcoming this.

'You know,' she said huskily, 'some people would dream of this. They'd say we were being unreasonable. Suddenly you're an important man with a great inheritance. Why aren't we glad?'

'Because it's a nightmare,' he said. 'Me, a count. The country bumpkin, which is all I've ever wanted to be. Do you want to be a contessa?'

'Are you kidding? I'd rather be a cow-pat.'

They clung together, seeking reassurance from each other, but each knowing they were fighting something that could suffocate them.

There was a knock on the door, and Dulcie looked in.

'Your uncle wants you in his study,' she said to Leo. 'He's got papers to show you.'

'Hell!'

'Best get it over with,' she said sympathet-
ically.

When he'd gone Selena said, 'How do you
feel about this? You were going to be a contessa, and now you're not. How can you
smile?'

Dulcie laughed and shrugged. 'I've had
enough of titles to last me a lifetime. Being a
countess never made my mother happy.'

'Your mother—is a countess?' Selena echoed.

'My father's an earl, that's a sort of English
count.'

'And you live—like this?' Selena indicated
their surroundings.

'Goodness no!' Dulcie laughed. 'We never
had two pennies to rub together. My father
gambled it all away. That's why I had to work
as a private detective. I couldn't do anything
else. Having a title doesn't qualify you for a
proper job.' She looked at Selena, suddenly
alert. 'Selena, what's the matter? Are you ill?'

'No, I'm not ill, but I've stepped into a crazy
house.'

Another knock on the door. This time it was
Harriet, and behind her a servant with a trolley

bearing champagne. While Dulcie began to pour, Harriet stretched out on a sofa and kicked off her shoes.

'Bubble, bubble, toil and trouble,' she said. 'You—*would—not—believe* the commotion that's going on downstairs.'

'We would,' Dulcie chuckled, handing the other two a glass each. 'We're well out of it.'

'Leo and Guido were practically coming to blows,' Harriet said cheerfully. 'Leo says he's going to wring Guido's neck. Oh, by the way, Liza would have come with me, but she's a little tired, and she's gone to bed. Actually I think it's her English that's troubling her. She doesn't speak it very well and she's afraid you may be offended.' This last was to Selena.

So that was the countess's excuse, Selena thought glumly. That was how these people operated. No outright snub, nothing you could take offence at. Just a half-truth that left you clutching at shadows.

She downed the champagne, which she suddenly needed badly.

Leo waited until the house was quiet before he slipped out of his room. Propriety be blowed, tonight he needed to be with Selena.

But when he opened her door he found her bed empty and no sign of her. He switched on the light to be sure, then switched it off again and went to the window. The Grand Canal lay before him, silent, mysterious, melancholy in its beauty. Many a man would envy him, the inheritor of all this, but it was his wide, rolling acres that called to him.

And his instincts told him that there was another trouble coming, and that was the one he dreaded.

Something caught his eye and he looked to see where the palace made a right angle to itself. Through the large windows he could see a white shape wandering through the great rooms.

Like any self-respecting palace this one had its ghosts, but none like this. Leo left the room quickly and hurried down through the building, across the marble floors that echoed the lightest footsteps.

He found the ghost in the ballroom, walking forlornly along the huge windows that went from floor to ceiling. All around them shone decorations of gold leaf. Above them hung gigantic crystal chandeliers, silent in the gloom.

He spoke her name softly, and she turned to look at him. Even in this light he could see her face well enough to know that it was distraught. The next moment they'd thrown themselves into each other's arms.

'I can't do it,' she cried. 'I just can't do this.'

'Of course you can,' he soothed her, stroking her hair although his heart was full of fear. 'You can do anything you set your mind to. I know that, even if you don't.'

'Oh, sure, I can do anything that takes grit and bull-headedness, but this—it would crush me.'

That was what he'd been afraid of. But he wasn't ready to give up.

'We wouldn't be trapped here all the time—'

'We would in the end.' She pulled away from him and began to pace restlessly. 'Look at this room. Dulcie would be at home here because she was raised in a place like this. Harriet would be all right because it's full of antiques. But me? I just spend my whole time hoping I don't bump into things.'

'It would be different in time,' he pleaded. 'You'll change—'

'Maybe I don't want to change,' she flashed at him. 'Maybe I think there's nothing wrong with the way I am.'

'I didn't say—'

'No, and you never will. But the truth is the truth, whether anyone says it or not. Leo, we don't just come from different worlds. It's different planets, different universes. You know it yourself.'

'We've overcome that before.'

'Yes, because of the farm. Because of the land, and the animals, and all the things we both love. It didn't matter where we came from, because we were heading in the same direction. But now—' she looked around her in despair.

'We don't have to spend much time here— we'll still have the farm—'

'Will we? This was going to be Guido's inheritance, and now he's lost it to you. Aren't you going to have to give him yours in exchange?'

That thought had been nibbling uneasily at the edge of his consciousness.

'Guido's not interested in farming, I can repay him in money. And if I have to I'll sell some of the antiques in this place. Every single one if I have to.'

'And we live on the farm and let your ancestral palace stand empty? Even I know better than that.' She tore at her short hair. 'If it was anywhere else you could simply move into the palace and buy up some farming land around it, but what can you do in Venice?'

'*Carissima*, please—'

'Don't call me that,' she said quickly.

'Why, suddenly—now?'

'Because everything's changed—now.'

'So suddenly I can't tell you that I love you more than life? I can't say that I don't want this either, but it'll be bearable if I have you?'

'*Don't!*' She turned away, her hands over her ears.

'Why mustn't I say that your love is everything to me?' he asked in a voice that was suddenly hard. 'Because you can't say the same?'

In the long silence that followed Leo felt his heart almost stop.

'I don't know,' she whispered at last. 'Oh, Leo, forgive me, but I don't know. I—I do love you—'

'Do you?' he asked in a harder voice than she had ever heard him use.

'Yes, I do love you, I do, I do—' With every repetition she grew more frantic. 'Please try to understand—'

'I understand this—that you only love me on certain conditions. When things get tough, suddenly the love isn't enough.'

He gave a bitter laugh. 'It's ironical isn't it? If I lost every penny I could count on your love. If I was left to starve in the streets I know you'd starve with me and never complain.'

'Yes—yes—'

'If I had to sell the shirt off my back you'd sell the shirt off yours, and we'd fight the world together and be happy. But if I'm rich, that means trouble. You turn away from me and wonder if I'm worth loving.'

'It's not like that,' she cried.

'I'm the same man, rich or poor, but you can only love me if we have the life you want. But I want that life too. I don't want all this either.'

'Then leave it. Tell them you won't accept. Let's go back to the farm and be happy.'

'You don't understand. It can't be done like that. All this is now my responsibility, to my family, to the people who work for us and depend on us. I can't just turn my back on all that.'

He took her gently by the shoulders and looked into her face. 'My darling, it's still a fight, just a different one. Why can't you stand by me in this one, as you would have done the other?'

'Because we'd each be fighting a different enemy, and we'd end up fighting each other. In a sense we already are.'

'This is just a little argument—'

'But you fired the first shot in the war a moment ago, didn't you notice? You said, "You don't understand". You're right. And as we go on there'll be a million things I don't understand, but you will. And more and more you won't understand the things that are important to me, and in the end we'll be saying "You don't understand" to each other a dozen times a day.'

They were silent with fear, each seeing the cracks in the ground beneath their feet that would soon become a chasm that love couldn't bridge.

But not yet. They couldn't face it just now.

'Don't let's talk any more tonight,' Leo said hurriedly. 'We're both in a state of shock. Let's leave it until we're calmer.'

'Yes, we'll do that. We'll talk when we get home.'

That put it at a safe distance. In the meantime they could hide from what was happening.

He took her back to her room and kissed her cheek at the door.

'Try to sleep well,' he said. 'We're going to need all our strength.'

As soon as she had closed the door he walked away. He hadn't tried to go in, and she hadn't said, 'Stay with me'.

Leo spent the next day closeted with his uncle, Guido and a brace of lawyers, while Dulcie and Harriet showed Selena Venice. For an hour she tried to make the right noises, but the

truth was the narrow alleys and canals suffo-
cated her.

They went into St Mark's where Dulcie and
Guido had married recently, and where Harriet
and Marco would marry soon.

It was like being an ant, Selena thought,
looking up into the ancient, echoing building.
It was magnificent, splendid, beautiful. But it
turned you into an ant.

She thought of the little parish church at
Morenza, and was glad that her own wedding
would be there, and not in this place that
crushed her.

Dulcie seemed to understand, for as they left
she took a close look at Selena's face and said,
'Come with me,' and shepherded them both to
the nearby landing stage, where there were
vaporetti, the boats Venetians used as buses.

'Three to the Lido,' she told the man in the
ticket booth. To Harriet and Selena she said,
'We're going to spend the rest of the day on
the beach.'

Selena's spirits had perked up as the boat
headed out for the forty-minute journey across
the wide lagoon. After all those alleys she was
in the open at last. And when they reached the

Lido, the long thin island that bounded the lagoon and boasted one of the best beaches in the world, she caught her first ever glimpse of the sea, and it cheered her even more. Now that was some open space!

They bought bathing costumes and towels in the beach shops. When they'd changed they hired a huge umbrella and sat beneath it, rubbing each other with sun cream. Dulcie told of the day she'd come here with Guido.

'He rubbed me with sun cream and I still managed to get burned, so he took me to his little bachelor flat and I was poorly for days.' She smiled reminiscently. 'It was very romantic.'

'But if you were poorly—' Selena said.

'He looked after me wonderfully.'

'But you didn't—he didn't—?'

'No. We didn't. That's what made it so romantic.'

Later they ran down the beach to swim in the sea. Selena loved it. All work and no play had been the pattern of her life, and fooling around in the sun and the waves with no purpose but to enjoy herself was a novel experience. She began to think there might be something to be said for Venice after all.

But when the day was over and it was time to return, the great palace seemed to loom, waiting to swallow her up. It was actually very well lit, with huge windows that let in the light, but in her present mood the shades seemed to fall on her as soon as she entered.

She found Leo depressed but resigned.

'There's no way out,' he said. 'I've spent the day looking over my future with lawyers and accountants until my eyes have crossed. They're trying to work out a way for me to compensate Guido financially, without having to sell the farm.'

'Can it be done?'

'If I spread it over several years.'

'How is Guido about that?'

'Great. He just shrugged and said, ''It's cool. Whatever.'' He doesn't care. He's so happy to have dumped it on me that he's like a kid out of school. And behind that juvenile charm he's a very astute businessman. What he really lives off is his souvenir business and it's making him a fortune. But of course I've got to do the right thing by him.'

'And you'll keep the farm?'

'Yes, but life's going to change for us.'

She nodded. 'For *us*. Maybe I should have been in there too instead of being sent off to play.'

'I don't think anyone was trying to exclude you, it's just that we were all talking Italian, and you wouldn't have understood.'

He could have bitten his tongue off as soon as he said the last words, but she only smiled and said, 'Sure.'

'I mean, neither the lawyer nor the accountant speak any English, so we'd have been translating—'

'It's all right. You were absolutely right. It doesn't really concern me, does it?'

'Everything that happens to me concerns you,' he said emphatically. 'I'm sorry, darling, maybe you should have come in, despite the practical problems.'

She nodded, still smiling but still keeping her distance. But his face looked so desperate and weary that she couldn't stand it.

'I'm sorry,' she said huskily, throwing her arms around him. 'I'm a bitch to nag you when you're unhappy.'

'Just stay with me,' he said, holding her tight. 'Don't leave me to struggle through this alone.'

'I won't, I won't.'

He sighed. 'I've got a confession to make. Uncle started on again about our wedding. According to him it has to be St Mark's. I told him it was up to you.'

'Oh, great! Blame me!' She managed to smile. 'You'd better say yes. You can't start your new life by fighting with your family.'

'Thank you *carissima*.' He held her fiercely. 'We'll be out of here tomorrow.'

'It'll be all right when we're home,' she insisted.

But her words sounded hollow even to her own ears. She was full of dread, and she could sense that his own dread matched it.

She kept repeating to herself that everything would be all right when they were away from here. It was a mantra that kept her going as they packed their things next morning. Just a few more hours, a few more minutes— Even then she knew there was no real escape. They would have to return in a couple of weeks for Leo to sign papers.

'You come alone,' she told him.

'I want you with me. After all, you said yourself that it concerns you too.'

'But there's nothing for me to sign. I'll stay home and—'

'And be there when I get back?' he asked fiercely. 'Will you?'

'Of—of course I will.'

'I want you with me,' he repeated with a hint of mulishness around his mouth.

So he sensed it too, she thought.

It was like an ugly demon sitting on the floor between them, forcing them both to side-step, but without ever admitting that it was there.

More than anyone it was the countess who unsettled her. Her English was so poor that they couldn't communicate except through an interpreter, and then Selena didn't know how to interpret her awkwardness. It might be shyness, unease, or downright disapproval. Selena reckoned she could guess which one.

In the last few minutes before they left the countess approached her. There was nobody else there, and in her hand she clutched a dictionary.

'I speak—with you,' she said in a voice that showed she was reciting prepared words.

'Yes?' Selena tried to look composed.

'Things are—different now—your marriage—we must speak—'

'But I know,' Selena said passionately. 'You don't have to tell me, I know. How can I marry him? You don't want me to, and you're right. I don't belong here. I don't belong in your world. *I know.*'

A tense, haughty look came over the countess's face. She took a sharp breath. The next moment there was the sound of footsteps on marble and she stepped back.

The rest of the family appeared, engulfing them. There were goodbyes, attempts at cheer. The boat was at the landing stage, then they were drawing away, the strip of water growing wide, and the problems were just beginning.

CHAPTER ELEVEN

Now there was the relief of attending to the harvest. All over the valley the vineyards and the olive groves were humming with activity. Carts passed along the lines, gradually filling up with the best the earth had to offer. Selena was there, sometimes with Leo, sometimes alone. Even alone she could communicate with Leo's people for most of them had a smattering of English and she had mastered a few words of Tuscan, which she used badly enough to amuse everyone. In this way she forged her links with them.

And it might all be for nothing, she would think, looking out over the acres as the sun descended. For who knew how things would be this time next year? Who knew how much of the farm would still belong to him? And these new friends she was making, with whom she felt so much more at ease than her fine new family in their grandiose palace, how many of them would still think of her as a friend?

They too were worried, she sensed it. They would stop and ask her questions, because she was going to marry the *padrone*, and therefore she must know him best. How could she tell them that she didn't feel she knew him at all any more? The instinctive fellow-feeling that had united her with Leo increasingly seemed no more than a happy memory.

And besides, she saw him less because he was constantly being recalled to Venice to settle some point or other. He'd sworn it would make very little difference to them, but by now they both knew that it wasn't in his power to keep that promise. Inch by inch he was being forced onto a road where she couldn't follow.

These days she often slept in her own room to hide the fact that she sometimes awoke gasping for breath. She had a sense of floundering in a maze from which there was no way out, but only roads growing narrower until they vanished altogether, and herself with them.

She called the Four-Ten, and avidly drank in news about the Hanworth family. Paulie had

gone to Dallas to start another internet firm—
or so he said, but Barton confided that a jealous husband had been haunting the ranch for
a while, uttering dire threats should Paulie ever
reappear.

Billie was marrying her guy, Carrie was ex-
ercising Jeepers, and they'd had two offers for
him. If Selena wasn't coming back—

'No,' Selena said quickly. 'If I'm not sending you enough money for him—'

'You're sending more than enough,' Barton
boomed, offended. 'Think I grudge you a little
horse feed?'

'I know you don't. You've all been such
good friends to me, but I'm not going to take
advantage of it—'

'What else are friends for? You don't want
me to sell Jeepers? He's a good racer and he's
going to waste right now.'

'I know but—just hang onto him a little
longer, please Barton. How's Elliot?'

'He's fine. Carrie rides him, and she says
he's a real sweet old feller.'

'Yes,' Selena said. 'I remember that.'

She hung up, and went into the kitchen to
discuss the evening meal with Gina. Leo was

due back from Venice and Gina was preparing sardine and potato bake for him. After that Selena went into the office and worked hard on paperwork for the horse farm.

Then she dropped her head on her hands and wept.

It was dark when Leo drove up, for the nights were drawing in. He ate his meal with gusto but when Selena asked about his trip he had strangely little to say.

She knew what that meant. Bit by bit he was being drawn into their world, and he didn't know how to tell her.

After supper she headed back to the office, to 'finish some stuff.'

'Aren't you coming to bed?' he asked.

'Well, I just thought I'd—'

'No,' he said. 'Come to bed.'

Arms about each other they climbed the stairs. In his room he took her in his arms and kissed her deeply. The desire was always there, perhaps deeper now that it was almost the only way they could communicate. They undressed each other swiftly, eager for the union that was still perfect and in which there were no problems.

For a short, blissful time there was a hot urgency that swept everything before it. She called his name as if from a long distance, and tried to find comfort in his look of tender adoration. As passion faded into contentment she fell asleep with her head against him.

But as soon as she slept her surroundings changed. She was fighting her way through a thicket. She struggled but it was closing in on her, shutting out the air, suffocating her. She awoke, gasping for breath.

'*Carissima*—' Leo sat up and put on the bedside light. 'Wake up, wake up!'

She held him until the shaking stopped and he drew her close, stroking her hair.

'It's all right,' he murmured. 'I'm here. Hold on to me, it was only a dream.'

'I couldn't breathe,' she choked. 'Everything's closing in on me and I can't find a way through.'

'You've had that dream before, haven't you?' he said sadly. 'I've see you toss and turn and I know you're unhappy. And then the next night you've insisted on sleeping apart. But you never tell me. Why won't you let me share it?'

As though he didn't know the answer!

'It's nothing,' she said quickly. 'Just a dream. Hold me.'

They clung together until he asked quietly, 'Are you going to leave me?'

In the long silence he felt the darkness fall over his heart.

'No,' she said at last, 'I don't think so—but—I need to go back for a while. Just for a while—'

'Yes,' he said heavily, 'just for a while.'

He drove her to Pisa Airport next day. They were late arriving and the flight to Dallas had already been called.

'I'd better hurry then,' she said.

'Have you got everything?'

She gave an edgy little laugh. 'You keep asking me that. I guess I'll find I've left something important behind.'

He nodded. 'Yes.'

'Will passengers—?'

Suddenly he said, 'Selena, don't go.'

'I have to.'

'No, you don't. If you go, you won't come back. This is where we have to work it out. Don't go.'

'There's my flight.'

'*Don't go!* You know as well as I do what'll happen if you do.'

She faced him. 'I'm sorry—I'm sorry.' Tears were pouring down her face. 'I did try, but I just can't—Leo, I'm sorry—so sorry—'

He reached out but she slipped through his fingers. At the gate she turned back for a last look. She wasn't crying now, but the misery on her face reflected his own. For one moment he thought she would run back to him. But then she was gone.

Winter was a busy time in the souvenir business. Guido had decided on his lines for the following year and was busy showing his product to customers. In a couple of weeks he had a show so big that the only place for it was the Palazzo Calvani. The count had grumbled at the 'indignity' but given his consent.

But in the midst of his preparations Guido found the time to take off for Rome, with Dulcie, to share their great news.

After two days in Rome, celebrating with Marco and Harriet, now in countdown to their wedding, and Lucia, who was in seventh heaven, they headed for Bella Podena.

'So I'm going to be an uncle,' Leo said, toasting them.

It was the fifth time he'd done so. Everyone in the household had toasted them the first time, and the proud parents-to-be were sitting in a glow of happiness.

But Dulcie was a little uncomfortable with her own joy. She'd sensed something forced about Leo's celebrating. When they were taking plates out into the kitchen, Gina having gone to bed, she touched his arm and asked gently, 'Is there any news?'

He shook his head. There was a heaviness about him that hurt her, because it was so unlike the cheerful, take-life-as-it-comes Leo that they all knew.

'She'll come back,' she said gently. 'It's not long—'

'One month, one week and three days,' he said simply.

'Do you know where she is?'

'Yes, I've started tracking her through the internet again. She's doing well.'

'You haven't spoken to her?'

'I called her once. She was very nice.' There was a heaviness in his voice that told Dulcie all she needed to know about that call.

'Call her again and tell her to come home,' Dulcie said firmly.

But Leo shook his head. 'It has to be how she wants. I can't take her freedom away from her.'

'But we all lose our freedom for the one we love. Some of it, anyway.'

'Yes, and that's fine, if it's given up gladly. But if it's coerced it can't work. If she doesn't come back to me of her own free will, she won't stay.'

'And if she doesn't come back because she doesn't know how badly you want her?'

Leo gave a painful smile. 'She knows that.'

'Oh, Leo!'

She put her arms around him, hugging tightly. He hugged her back, dropping his shaggy head to rest on her shoulder, where she stroked it tenderly.

Guido, coming into the kitchen with plates, stopped on the threshold.

'My wife in my brother's arms!' he announced. 'Should I be jealous, creep away, shoot myself?'

'Oh, stop your nonsense!' his wife ordered him.

'Yes, dear!'

Dulcie gave Leo a little shake. 'It's going to be all right.'

'Of course it is,' he replied.

'He didn't mean a word of it,' Dulcie told her husband as they prepared for bed. 'It's not all right for him at all. He's living in a half-world. Gina told me today that sometimes he stands at the window looking down the road where he first saw her. It's as though he expected her to appear again, as if by magic. Just like last time.'

'Drat the woman!' Guido said, getting into bed and curving his arm for her. 'What does she mean by doing this to him?'

'Don't let Leo hear you say a word against her,' Dulcie advised, snuggling up to her husband. 'He understands her. He says she must find her own way home. If she doesn't, it means it's not really her home.'

'That's very profound for Leo,' Guido said, much struck. 'His mind never used to rise above the very basic—horses, crops and willing ladies, not necessarily in that order.'

'But he's changed. Even I've seen that, and I didn't really know the old Leo. I'll tell you this, Leo reckons her feelings are more important than his own.'

'I wish *I* did.' Guido sighed. 'The truth is, I suppose I'm feeling guilty. If I'd left well alone—?'

'What else could you do? The records were there. They have to work their own salvation out.'

'And if they fail—? What's that noise?' He rose and went to the window, looking out at a high barn, from which came the sound of a voice, coaxing and pleading. A faint light shone from one of the windows.

'It sounds like Leo,' he said, pulling on a dressing gown. 'What's he playing at? He's supposed to be in bed.'

Dulcie paused long enough to put on her own dressing gown, then followed her husband down to the yard and across to the barn. The door stood open.

Inside, the hay was piled up to the high ceiling just below which there was a ledge. A ladder stood propped against one of the supports, with Leo climbing unsteadily to the top, which fell several feet short of the ledge.

'Leo, whatever's the matter up there?' Guido yelled.

'It's a barn owl. She's trapped. I think she's hurt her wing.'

'Isn't she safe up there?'

Leo's voice reached him faintly. 'She can't fly for food, and she has young. I'm trying to bring them all down to safety.'

'Careful,' Guido called his alarm. 'It's dangerous. Haven't you got a longer ladder?'

'It's being mended. I'm all right. Just a little further.'

Leo had reached the top now, so that he was on a level with the birds. Guido, watching below, could see a white owl face in the gloom.

'Is he all right?' Dulcie asked, coming to stand beside her husband.

'Well, he's got rocks in his head, but that's nothing new,' Guido said with a shrug that was

pure Venetian in its mixture of humour, res-
ignation, affection and wryness.

'He's risking a terrible fall,' Dulcie said
worriedly. 'For an owl?'

'The way he sees it, it's his owl. Whatever's
his he looks after.'

A low whisper of triumph overhead announced that Leo had succeeded, at least. He
was holding the injured barn owl in one hand,
and supporting himself with the other, moving
back very carefully, unable to see where he
was going.

'How near am I to the ladder?' he yelled.

'Another three feet,' Guido called. 'But you
can't do it with one hand full.'

Guido was level with the ladder now. Gently
Leo laid the owl down in the hay and began
to lower himself, his feet seeking the top rung.
When he'd found it he reached back for the
owl, but the nervous creature suddenly took
fright and began to flutter awkwardly, moving
just out of reach.

'Don't be difficult, *cara*,' Leo pleaded. 'Just
a few minutes and we'll both be safe.'

'Leave it,' Dulcie pleaded from below. 'It's
too dan— *Leo*!'

The owl had edged back, causing Leo to lunge after it. It all happened in a flash. He lost contact with the ladder, tried frantically to regain his footing, and the next moment was plunging to the ground.

After Dallas Selena's next move should have been to Abilene, where she'd always done well. But by giving Abilene a miss she was able to head back to Stephenville, and the chance to see Elliot.

She'd formed a bond with Jeepers that went deeper than she could have believed possible. But Elliot was her family. He'd been with her through the times when she didn't have two cents to rub together. The way she saw it, he'd introduced her to Leo.

She didn't quite admit to herself that it was also a chance to see the Hanworths, and talk about Leo. She was working on being strong and sensible about that. Since she'd made the decision to cut him out of her life it was pure self-indulgence to revel in talking about him.

But if the subject happened to come up it would do a little to ease the ache in her heart that was with her, night and day. The temptation to stay with him had been overwhelming. She'd fought it as much for his sake as her own. To be with him year after year, failing him, never quite understanding the things that mattered in his world, and to see the disillusion appearing in his eyes—these things would have been unendurable.

He would have been kind, she had no doubt of that. As the dimensions of his mistake became clear to him he would have become increasingly gentle, determined not to blame her for the disaster he had urged on her. And it would have been his kindness that broke her heart.

Several times she started to dial his number, but she always managed to be strong in time, and hang up with the number incomplete.

It was nearly dark when she reached the Four-Ten, later than she'd intended because she'd stopped twice on the way, trying to decide if she was really going or not. There were lights on in the house, but at the sound of her engine a dozen more came on. The front door was thrown open and Barton came hurrying out to greet her.

'Get inside fast,' he said tensely. 'Leo's brother's here.'

'Barton, has something happened?'

'Guido will tell you. Hurry!'

She didn't know how she got inside. Guido was there. He rose to his feet as she appeared and her heart nearly failed her, for she had never seen a face so pale and distraught.

'Guido, what's happened?'

'Leo had a fall,' he said, and stopped as though he couldn't bear to go on.

'And?' she repeated in agony.

'He was up high in the barn, chasing after a hurt owl—you know what he's like—and he missed his footing and fell—best part of forty feet.'

'Oh, God! Please Guido, tell me he's alive.'

'Yes, he is, but we don't know when he'll walk again.'

Her hands flew to her mouth. Leo, the man who never sat when he could stand, never walked when he could run; Leo in a wheelchair, or worse. She turned away so that Guido couldn't see that she was fighting not to cry.

'I came to take you home,' Guido said. 'He needs you, Selena.'

'Of course. Oh, why didn't you just telephone me? I could have been on my way.'

'To be honest, I didn't think you'd be willing. I came here to take you by force if I had to.'

'Of course she'll come,' Barton said, entering from the hall. 'You leave everything here, Selena. Elliot and Jeepers will be just fine with us. Get going, girl.'

He drove them to the airport himself. Guido already had her air tickets.

'I told you I wasn't going to take no for an answer,' he said with a wan smile. 'I meant it.'

'You really thought I wouldn't come if Leo needs me?'

'I don't think you'd have believed a phone call. It's just words coming from a long way away.'

'But you came all this way for me,' she said, softened.

'I had to. I don't know how he's going to be, but I do know you've got to be there.'

He dozed most of the journey, and Selena didn't care to talk. Too many thoughts were confusing her all at once. She wouldn't know what she thought until she saw Leo again.

From Pisa Airport a car conveyed them to the hospital. Selena's nails ground into her palm. Now the moment had come she was terrified at what she would find. The last few yards to Leo's ward seemed endless.

His door was just in front of them. Guido opened it and stood back to let her go in.

Her eyes went swiftly to the bed, and then she stopped, frozen.

There was nobody there.

'Selena?'

The voice came from the window. She turned and saw a man standing there supported by crutches, one leg in plaster.

'Selena?' He made an unsteady, hobbling step towards her, and the next moment she was in his arms.

It was an awkward kind of kiss, holding each other up, not daring to clasp too tight, but it was the sweetest they had ever known.

'How do you come to be here?' he managed to say at last, when he could speak.

'That—brother of yours—'

Leo gave a shaky laugh. 'Has he been up to his tricks again?'

'*You!*' From the safety of Leo's arms Selena turned on Guido, watching them with immense satisfaction, from the doorway. 'You told me he couldn't walk.'

'Well, he can't walk,' Guido said innocently. 'That's why he's got crutches. He broke his ankle.'

'He broke—?'

'Any other man would have been killed by that fall,' Guido added. 'But the devil looks after his own, and Leo landed on a bale of hay.'

He vanished tactfully.

'You came back to me,' Leo said huskily. 'Hold me tightly.'

She did so and he immediately winced.

'It doesn't matter,' he said. 'All that matters is that you're back, and you're staying. Yes, you are—' he said it quickly before she could argue. 'You're not going to leave me again, I couldn't bear it.'

'I couldn't bear it either,' she said fervently. 'It was so dreadful without you. I kept trying to believe I'd done the right thing, then I'd weaken and decide to follow you, but then I'd be afraid of embarrassing you because you'd probably found somebody else—'

'You stupid, stupid woman,' he said lovingly.

He winced again at he spoke.

'Come on,' she said tenderly, 'you should be in bed.'

With his arm around her shoulders he hobbled the few steps to the bed, where she helped him off with his robe. Beneath it his chest was bare, except for some strapping, and she gasped at the multitude of bruises, blue, black, red, overlapping each other.

'It's all right, they're getting better,' he said.

Clinging to her he eased himself down onto the bed and lay back, exhausted.

'If you could pull the sheet up—Selena? Don't cry.'

'I'm not crying,' she wept, trying to brush back the tears that flowed down her cheeks.

'You're not?' he asked tenderly.

'No, I'm not. You know I never cry, and don't you dare try to suggest—oh, look at you! Oh, my darling, darling—'

He held her as close against him as he dared, kissing the top of her head.

'It looks worse than it is,' he reassured her. 'Just a few bruises—well, OK, a cracked rib or two, but nothing to what it might have been.'

Guido slid out of the door, unnoticed by either of them.

'I never thought I'd see you again,' Leo said. 'It's like a dream come true. How could you leave me?'

'I don't know. But I never will again.'

He was home in a week, promising the doctor to go straight to bed, and spending the first day in the car while Selena drove him over his lands.

'Now you're going to bed, as you promised,' she said firmly when they got home.

'Only if you come with me.'

'You're not well enough.'

'I'm well enough to hold you against my heart,' he said. 'That's what I've missed the most. Don't you know that?'

He was still a very odd colour but he moved more easily, and when he'd settled into bed he was able to put his arms about her without wincing too much.

'Are you going to be all right for the journey next week?' she asked.

'Sure, Venice is no distance, and I wouldn't miss seeing Marco's wedding for anything. And don't worry, just because they're marrying in St Mark's, that doesn't mean that people will start nagging us to do the same. They understand that we'll be marrying here.'

He sighed. 'It can't be soon enough for me. We might go down to the church and talk about it tomorrow.'

Silence.

'*Carissima*? Is something the matter?'

'Don't let's rush anything, Leo.'

'Well, I can't rush anything, can I? Look at me. I need to get fully fit because I want to enjoy our wedding day, but that won't take long—'

'No, that's not what I mean.' She sat up, evading his hand that would have drawn her back.

'Leo, I do love you, please believe that. And now that I've come back I won't go away again. It hurt too much. But in a sense, nothing has changed. The things that were wrong before are still wrong now.

'I won't leave you, I swear it, but—I can't marry you.'

CHAPTER TWELVE

FOR breakfast Gina had a wide choice of dishes, each one a favorite of Leo's, which she pressed on him until he begged for mercy.

'I'll clear away, Gina,' Selena said. 'I know you've got masses to do.'

'*Si, signorina.*' Gina nodded and went on her way.

'That's it,' Leo said when she'd gone. 'Gina's accepted you as her employer. As far as she's concerned it's a done deal.'

'Gina's flattering me. I wouldn't know how to run a house and she knows it even better than I do.'

'Of course. That's her job. Your job is to leave everything to her. But haven't you noticed that these days she asks you, not me?' He rested his fingertips on the back of her hand. 'Signora Calvani,' he murmured.

'Leo—I told you last night—'

'I was hoping that was a nightmare,' he groaned. 'You went away so soon afterwards—'

'You weren't saying anything.'

'I was trying to pretend it hadn't happened. Selena, please let's forget last night. After everything that's happened we weren't our normal selves.' When she shook her head he demanded, 'Are you trying to send me white haired?'

'I can't marry you. I couldn't be a countess if my life depended on it. Your uncle won't live for ever. What happens when you inherit? One day you'll want to do the whole "count thing" properly, Venice, the palace, society, the whole lot.'

'*Me?*' he demanded aghast. 'Selena, for pity's sake, I'm a country man. You can't rear horses in Venice. They'd drown.'

But the attempt at a joke fell on stony ground. Selena's face was as stubborn as he'd ever seen it, and he was filled with alarm.

'I don't believe this,' he said. 'I thought we'd settled that we loved each other and were going to be together for ever. Or did I miss something?'

'No, my darling, I do love you. Oh, Leo, if you knew how much I love you. I'll stay, but not like that.'

'Well that's too bad, because *like that* is how I am,' he snapped.

He spoke more harshly than she ever heard him before, but his nerves were taut. His head was aching, his foot was aching, and his normal resilience was at a low ebb.

'But it can't be how *I* am,' she said, setting her chin.

And suddenly the chasm was there again, as though they had never been reunited.

They papered over the cracks to drive to Venice for the wedding. There they smiled and played their roles perfectly. The palace had only just got back to normal after Guido's trade show, before it was snowed under with guests for the wedding.

Selena was glad to vanish into the crowd. She and Leo had agreed not to alert the family to their differences, and there were a few of the usual hints about setting the date. But they could cope with these more easily than the truth.

And she knew that Leo was hoping that if nothing was said, her resolution would simply wear out.

In the great basilica of St Mark's she watched the bride arrive, and knew that Harriet was at home in these grand surroundings. There was a magnificence about her as she gave her hand to the man she loved, and he looked at her out of eyes full of emotion. Their happiness seemed to fill the church and reach out to touch everyone there.

Selena turned and met Leo's eyes. She was sure she saw reproach in them, as though he was accusing her of denying him the same happiness. She looked away. Why couldn't he understand that she was doing what was best for both of them?

At the reception she drank champagne, toasted the bride and groom and cheered them when they left on honeymoon. As the evening wore on she looked around for Leo, but he'd vanished into the count's study with some of the other men. And he stayed there until she'd gone to bed.

Next day he was subdued during the farewells, and on the journey home he dozed while she drove. They left late and it was dark when they reached home. Selena had told Gina to go to bed, and they found supper waiting for them.

As they uncovered the dishes she said, 'You told them, didn't you?'

'I didn't need to. They could tell. They kept asking me about our wedding, and you can only put people off just so often before they guess the truth.'

'So now they know. Perhaps it's best.'

'Selena, didn't anything that happened back there mean anything to you? Didn't you see Marco and Harriet, the way they committed themselves to each other? That's why marriage is important. Without it there's no commitment. I thought we were committed, but now you're telling me that you're not. What kind of a future can we have?'

'We'll make our future in our own way—'

'In your way, you mean? I love you, I want you for my wife.'

'It's impossible,' she said despairingly.

'It's only impossible if you make it so.' He took a deep breath. 'What's impossible to me is to go on like this.'

'What are you saying?'

'I'm saying that I love you, and I'm proud of you. I want to walk out of church with you on my arm and tell the world this is the woman I've chosen, and she's chosen me. I hope you wanted the same, but if you don't—'

'Go on.'

He said, as though the words were torn out of him, 'If you don't, then we have nothing. You may as well go home again.'

'Are you throwing me out, Leo?'

Suddenly he slammed his hand on the table, and in this sweet-tempered man the gesture was more shocking than it would have been in anyone else.

'No, dammit!' he roared. 'I want you to stay here. I want you to love me, and marry me and have my children. I want to spend the rest of my life with you. But it has to be *married*. Does that sound like throwing you out?'

'It sounds like giving me an ultimatum.'

'All right then, I'm giving you one. If you love me one tenth as much as you've always said you do, then marry me. I can't compromise on this, it's too important to me.'

'And what about what's important to me?'

'I've heard about nothing except what's important to you, and I've tried to understand, although it put me through hell. Now it's my turn to tell you what I want.'

She stared at him, a man she'd thought she knew through and through. Leo had finally lost his temper, not in the half humorous way she'd seen when he roared with frustration, but in deep, genuine anger. His eyes were as gleaming and dangerous as any man's she'd ever seen. It was as though the last piece of him had slid into place.

That feeling persisted even when he immediately ran his hand through his hair and said, 'I'm sorry. I didn't mean to shout.'

'I don't mind shouting,' she said truthfully. 'I can always shout back. I'm good at that.'

'Yes, I know,' he said shakily. 'I don't mind the shouting either. It's the silent distances I can't stand.'

'There are too many of them now,' she agreed.

She took a step towards him. He moved in the same moment, and they were in each other's arms.

It was a long, fulfilling kiss and she felt her fears and tensions ease. While they had this—

'Don't ever frighten me like that again,' she said. 'I really thought you meant it.'

He released her. 'I did mean it.'

She stepped back. 'No, Leo, please—listen—'

'I've listened as much as I mean to,' he said firmly. 'I can't do it your way. In here—' he touched his heart '—you're already my wife. I can't live differently on the outside. I can't live a divided life.'

'And you'd really send me away?'

'My darling, if we tried to do it your way we'd pull apart sooner rather than later, and part miserably. We'd have nothing left but bitter memories. It would be better to part now, while there's still love to remember.'

'*Oh, you*—'

She turned away, waving her arms in angry, helpless gestures, then began to bang her head against the wall. He quickly took hold of her and pulled her away, pressing her against him.

'I feel like doing that too,' he said, 'but it just gives you a headache.'

'What are we going to do?' she wept.

'We're going to have something to eat, and we're going to talk like civilised people.'

But they couldn't talk. They had each stated their position, and each recognised that the other was immovable. What was there to say after that?

They were both glad to go to bed, in their separate rooms, but after a couple of hours of lying awake Selena got dressed and came downstairs.

She didn't put any lights on, but walked from room to room in silence, wondering if she would soon leave here. It would have been so easy to run back to Leo and promise to marry him, anything rather than leave him. But the conviction that they would both pay a heavy price for a brief happiness lay heavy on her. She could take the risk for herself, but not for him.

She wanted to bang her head against the wall again, but she didn't because she was too tired and her head was aching already. At last she settled on a sofa by the window, put her arms on the back, and dozed off uneasily.

She was awoken by a hand on her shoulder.

'Darling, wake up,' Leo said.

'What time is it?' she asked, moving stiffly.

'Seven in the morning. We've got visitors, look.'

They went out into the yard, where two cars that they recognised were coming up the slope.

'It's the family,' she said. 'But we saw them only yesterday. Why have they followed us here?'

The cars drew to a halt, and Guido and Dulcie got out of the first. Out of the second, to their astonishment, stepped the count and countess.

'We are here on a very important matter,' Count Calvani announced. 'My wife insists that she must speak to Sclena. The rest of us merely travel as her entourage.'

'Come inside,' Leo said. 'It's too cold to stay out hcre.'

Inside Gina served them with hot coffee. Selena was still trying to sort out what was happening. Why did the old woman want to see her? Why were her eyes fixed on her so urgently?

'Will someone tell me what's happening?' she said.

'I come to you,' Liza said slowly, 'because there are things—' she hesitated, frowning '—things that only I can say.'

'We're here to help,' Dulcie said, 'in case Liza's English runs out. She's been working hard at learning it, for your sake, and as far as possible she wants to say this herself.'

'I tried before,' Liza said. 'But then—I do not have the words—and you do not listen.'

'When you were in Venice the first time,' Dulcie said. 'Liza tried to talk to you, but you ran away.'

'There was no need for her to tell me I was the wrong person for Leo,' Selena said. 'I knew that.'

'No, no, no!' Liza said firmly. She glared at Selena. 'You should talk less, listen more. *Si*?'

'*Si!*' Leo said at once.

Unexpectedly Selena also smiled. '*Si,*' she said.

'Good,' Liza spoke robustly. 'I come to say—you do a terrible thing—as I did. And you must not.'

'What am I doing that's terrible?' Selena asked cautiously.

'After what Leo told us we had a family conference last night,' Guido said, 'and we reckoned we all had to come out here and talk some sense into you. But Liza most of all.'

'Now, you come with me,' Liza said firmly. She set down her cup and headed for the door.

'Can I come?' Leo asked.

Liza regarded him. 'Can you keep quiet?'

'Yes, Aunt,' he said meekly.

'Then you can come.' She marched out.

'What is she doing?' Selena asked him.

'I think I know. You can trust her.'

He followed them out to the car, handing Liza in, while Dulcie got behind the wheel.

'Drive down through Morenza,' Liza said, 'and then—two miles further on—a farm.'

Dulcie followed instructions and they were soon out in the countryside, surrounded by fields, with the occasional low-roofed building. The others came behind them.

'There,' Liza said, indicating a farm house.

Dulcie turned in and drove the short distance to the cluster of buildings. A middle-aged man looked up and greeted Liza. Selena didn't hear the words they exchanged. Liza led the way past the house to a collection of out-buildings, and into a cow byre.

It was a large building, filled with animals, for they had arrived at milking time.

Liza turned and faced Selena.

'I was born here,' she said.

Selena frowned. 'You mean—in the house?'

'No, I mean here, in this room, where we stand now. My mother was a servant and she lived here, with the animals. In those days—it sometimes happened. Poor people lived like that. And we were very, very poor.'

'But—' Selena looked around helplessly.

'I was not born a fine lady. You didn't know?'

'Yes, I knew you weren't born with a title but—this—'

'Yes,' Liza nodded. 'This. In those days there was—big gap between rich and poor.' She demonstrated with her hands. 'And my mother was not married. She never told my father's name, and there was much disgrace for her. This was seventy years ago, you understand. Not like now.

'When I was a child—my mother died, and I was put to work in the house. Always I was told—I was lucky to have food and work. I was a bastard. I had no rights. I was taught nothing.

'It was Maria Rinucci who saved me. These lands—her dowry when she married Count Angelo Calvani. She was sorry for me—took me to Venice with her. That was how I met my Francesco.'

A glow came over her face as she turned to look at the count, watching her, smiling.

'If you could have seen him then,' she said, returning his smile, 'how young and handsome—he loved me, and of course I loved him. But—no use. He must marry—great lady. He ask me. I say no. How can he marry me? For forty years I say no. And then—I understand—I make big mistake. And now I come to tell you—don't make my mistake.'

'But Liza—' Selena stammered '—you don't know—'

'Don't be stupid,' Liza said flatly. 'Of course I know. I tell *you*. People think it must be—wonderful to be Cinderella. I say no. Sometimes—a burden.'

'Yes,' Selena said in relief at finding someone who understood. 'Yes.'

'But if it's your destiny,' Liza said fiercely, 'you must accept that burden—else you will break Prince Charming's heart.'

She took her husband's hand. He was looking at her with a world of love in his eyes.

'People see us and they think how romantic that our story had a happy ending,' Liza said, a little sadly. 'But what they do not see is in here—' she indicated her breast '—my bitter regret that our love was only fulfilled at the end. We could have been happy long ago, I could have had his children. But I wasted all those years because I made too much of things that didn't matter.'

Leo had come quietly forward until he was standing beside Selena. Liza saw it, and smiled.

She had one last thing to say to Selena, and now her words began to come easily, as though she had found the key.

'In all your life, nobody has valued you, and so you did not learn to value yourself. Then how can you understand Leo, who values you more than anything in the world? How can you accept his love, when you think you are not worthy of love?'

'Is that what I think?' Selena asked, dazed.
'Has anyone else ever loved you?'

Selena shook her head. 'No. Nobody.
You're right. You grow up thinking that you're
not entitled to much—' she saw Liza nod in a
comprehension that included only the two of
them '—and when Leo loved me I kept thinking he'd made a mistake, and he'd wake up
soon and realise that it was only me after all.'

'Only you,' Liza echoed. 'Only the woman
he adores. Only the first woman he has ever
asked to marry him. And, I think, the last.
Don't harm him as I harmed my Francesco.
But trust him. Trust his love for you. Trust
your own love for him. Don't make my mistake, and throw away your happiness until it
is almost too late.'

Selena turned to Leo and found him looking
anxiously into her face. The enormity of what
she'd nearly done to him shook her and she
couldn't stop the tears coming.

'I love you,' she said huskily. 'I love you
so much—and I never understood a thing.'

'You just didn't know about families,' he
said tenderly. 'Now you do.'

She was wanted. The whole family was opening its hearts and its arms to her—she, who'd never had kin that she could recall—not who'd wanted her, anyway.

'Marry me,' he said at once. 'Let me hear you say it.'

She never did say it. She could only nod vigorously while he took her into his arms and held her. Leaning down so that his chin rested on her head. Recovered treasure.

'I'm never letting you go again,' he said.

They set the wedding for as soon as possible, before winter closed in. Count Francesco was so delighted to be welcoming Selena into the family at last that he yielded about St Mark's, and happily agreed that the village church in Morenza was the only suitable place.

The date was booked at the little church, and a flurry of cleaning got the house ready for guests.

For the groom there was the entire Calvani family, but now they were Selena's family too. Selena had invited Ben, the loyal friend who'd kept her on the road long enough to meet Leo, and his wife, Martha. She sent them the tickets, and on the day she and Leo drove to the airport to collect them.

This wedding wouldn't have been complete without the Hanworths, all except Paulie, who found something better to do. Leo went to meet them alone, leaving Selena with Ben and Martha, catching up on old times.

'I'd better give you this before I forget it,' Selena said casually, handing Ben an envelope.

'How much?' Ben yelped at the size of the cheque he pulled out.

'That's all the money I must owe you going back a few years. Do you think I didn't know how you pared the bills down? And you couldn't afford it.'

'Can *you* afford it? You must have won every race in sight.'

'It's not all winnings. I'm working for Leo now, with his horses.'

'He pays you?'

'You bet he pays me. I'm very good at my job. I don't come cheap.'

'Well, I guess you found your right place. You always did have a way with horses. Look what you managed to do with Elliot. Nobody else could have done as well with him.'

'Oh, Ben, don't. The one thing that isn't perfect was that I just abandoned Elliot.'

'I thought he was being cared for by that Hanworth fellow who's coming this afternoon.'

'He is. He'll have the best of everything, but I just know he's wondering why I don't come back. Talking of coming back, where is everyone? Leo should have brought them home by now.'

As the day wore on Selena had the feeling that everyone was in on a secret from which only she was excluded. Maids giggled in doorways and vanished at her approach. Once Gina asked if Leo had given her a wedding present yet.

'Not yet,' Selena said, bewildered.

'Perhaps you get it today,' Gina observed, and went away smiling.

Hours passed. She began to feel nervous. Surely they should have been home by now?

In the late afternoon Gina came to find her.

'*Signorina*, I think you should look out of the window. There is something there for you to see.'

Puzzled, Selena went to look down the road that led to the village. A little group of people were walking slowly up to her. She recognised Barton, Delia and the rest of the family. But she also recognised a figure that she hadn't dared hope to see again.

'*Elliot!*' she shrieked and flew out of the house.

Leo was leading the way up the road, holding Elliot's bridle, grinning as he saw her. All the others were smiling too as she arrived in a rush and threw her arms about the old horse's neck.

'You—' she whirled on the Hanworth family. 'You brought him over with you?'

'Sure did,' Barton said, beaming. 'Me and Leo stitched it all up, and he swore he wouldn't let you get wind of it.'

Selena had remembered her manners and embraced Delia, Barton, then the girls. She would have hugged Jack too but he warned her off with a boyish glare.

'Elliot, Elliot—' Tears poured down her face.

'That's why we've been so long,' Leo said. 'It took time to get him off the plane and clear him for entry. Never seen so much paperwork, but in the end they passed him. By the way, that offer on Jeepers is still open.'

'Better take it,' Selena agreed. 'He's a racer, he needs to do his stuff. Elliot—' she kissed his nose again '—just needs to rest and be loved.'

The Calvanis arrived next day, and they and the Hanworths immediately took to each other. In the rowdy party that followed Selena saw Liza looking a little overwhelmed and took her up to bed.

'Thank you. Thank you for everything.'

When they had hugged she said, 'You really think I can do it—be a *contessa*?'

'Not in the old way,' Liza said. 'That belonged to another age. You will do it your own way, and that is right. Things must change if they are to live.'

Selena considered this. 'A cowgirl *contessa*?'

'I like that,' Liza said at once. 'I admired you so much at the rodeo. It's such a shame that I'm too old to learn to ride.' They laughed, then she became serious again. 'Only one thing makes you a *contessa*, and that is the love of a count. Never forget that.'

Downstairs Selena found the brothers arguing about money. Guido didn't want to take any from Leo, know that the raising of it might damage the farm.

'And who wants to live in the palace once you've sold off everything?' he demanded.

'I don't want to live in it at all,' Leo retorted. 'Uncle, please arrange to live a very long time so that this will remain academic.'

'I'll do my best,' the count agreed imperturbably, 'but when I'm not there this problem *will* be there. Still. You should settle it now.'

'I don't want to live in the palace,' Leo said stubbornly.

'Then we needn't,' Selena said. 'Guido can stay there.'

Everyone turned to look at her.

'Guido, have I got this right?' Selena asked him. 'You don't want the title and all the stuff that goes with it. But you love Venice, and you love the palace.'

'Right.'

'And it's a great backdrop for your business.' She turned to Leo. 'So he stays there.

We just have to turn up for special occasions. You work out the rent and discount it against the compensation. That way the palace isn't standing empty, and the money worries are sorted. Everyone's happy.'

In the silence the brothers looked at each other.

'She's a brilliant lady you're marrying,' Guido said with a grin.

'What did I tell you?' the count roared. 'I said the Calvanis always get the best wives,' he swung Selena around in a dance, *'and we've done it again.'*

The wedding was a true family occasion, with the family being the whole village. When Leo walked Selena out of the church and three times around the duck pond—because they always did that in Morenza—he started up the hill, followed by everyone in the village who could walk, and every tenant they had.

At the gate of the farmhouse the crowd gave them a rousing cheer before going back to the public hall where a spread was laid out for them. Leo would gladly have invited them all inside, but the house would have burst at the seams.

The sight of herself in bridal white with a flowing veil had taken Selena's breath away. She didn't look like the person she knew at all, but perhaps that was the way to start a new life. She wasn't sure who this person was, but she belonged to Leo body, heart and soul, because he had given her the same, and given it first.

She wondered what would have happened if Guido hadn't brought her back to Italy by subterfuge. As the party quietened down, she felt moved to remind her husband, 'I guess we owe a lot to Guido. If he hadn't been able to cook up a good story, none of us would be here.'

Leo raised his glass to his brother. 'I guess that's true.'

'It's in the blood of the Venetians,' Guido said cheerfully. He'd had a little too much champagne, or he would never have said the next words. 'We all have those little skills, inventing, forgery—'

There was a sudden silence, in which his last words seemed to echo.

'Forgery?' Leo repeated. 'What do you mean—forgery?'

The silence had taken on a stunned quality as the implications sank in. Everyone was looking at Guido.

Guido, who had discovered the evidence that made Leo legitimate. Guido, who had sworn he would escape the title, no matter what he had to do.

Guido—the master of tricks and spells, the man of masks and illusions, the *Venetian*.

'Oh, no!' Leo groaned. 'You wouldn't do that to me! Tell me you wouldn't.'

Guido looked at him, bland and innocent. 'Who me?'

'Yes, you, *brother*! You sneaky, tricky, unscrupulous—'

He set down his glass and began to advance on Guido, who backed off cautiously.

'Now, Leo, don't do anything you'll regret—'

'I won't regret anything I do to you.'

But he was checked by the last sound anyone there had expected to hear. Selena burst into peals of laughter. The others relaxed and began to smile as her mirth echoed around the room.

'Selena, *carissima*—'

'Oh, my goodness!' she choked. 'This will be the death of me! I haven't heard anything as good as this in years.'

'Well, I'm glad you find it funny—'

'It's your face that's funny, my darling.' She put her hands on either side of his head and kissed him, still laughing.

Her mirth was infectious. He couldn't help himself laughing with her, even through his dismay.

'But don't you realise what Guido's done to us?' he demanded. 'He forged that evidence.'

'Has he? Are you sure of that? He hasn't admitted it.'

'And he'll never tell you, one way or the other,' Marco observed, eyeing Guido judicially. 'But I'm betting he's innocent, although it pains me to find him innocent of anything.'

Guido ran a finger around his collar.

'What I think happened is this,' Marco continued. 'He got wind of the Vinelli marriage in England, and he employed an army of private investigators to hunt it down. After all, we have a P.I. in the family.' His amused eyes rested on Dulcie. 'I dare say she put him in touch with a few?'

Guido seized his wife's hand and muttered, 'Say nothing.'

'Very wise,' Marco continued. 'Well, that's my theory for what it's worth.'

'You think it's real?' Leo asked him. 'Not a forgery.'

'I doubt he forged anything, although he'll let you think he did, just to tease a rise out of you.'

'I'll break every bone in his body,' Leo said.

Guido hopped nimbly out of range. 'No violence,' he said. 'Remember I'm an expectant father.'

Marco said in Leo's ear, 'And that's where you'll get your revenge.'

'What do you mean?' the brothers demanded with one voice.

'Children tend to take the opposite tack to their fathers. It would serve Guido right if his son wanted all the things he was so glad to give up. When that day comes, he may have some explaining to do.'

'But you just said—he didn't forge it,' Leo reminded him.

'Well, I don't think even Guido would go that far.'

'But how can we be sure?' Leo groaned.

'Easy,' Marco said, 'you check the English register offices. I think you'll find it there.'

'But let's not do that,' Selena said. 'Let's not know. Then it's not boring and predictable any more.'

'Will I ever understand you?' Leo asked tenderly.

'You do,' she said simply. 'You've always understood me, when I never understood myself.'

She touched his face.

'I had the prize,' she said softly, 'and I nearly let it go. But I'll never let it go again. All my life, for ever and ever.'

MILLS & BOON® PUBLISH EIGHT LARGE PRINT TITLES A MONTH. THESE ARE THE EIGHT TITLES FOR DECEMBER 2003

———————— ❦ ————————

AT THE SPANIARD'S PLEASURE
Jacqueline Baird

SINFUL TRUTHS
Anne Mather

HIS FORBIDDEN BRIDE
Sara Craven

BRIDE BY BLACKMAIL
Carole Mortimer

RUNAWAY WIFE
Margaret Way

THE TUSCAN TYCOON'S WIFE
Lucy Gordon

THE BILLIONAIRE BID
Leigh Michaels

A PARISIAN PROPOSITION
Barbara Hannay

MILLS & BOON®

Live the emotion

MILLS & BOON® PUBLISH EIGHT LARGE PRINT TITLES A MONTH. THESE ARE THE EIGHT TITLES FOR JANUARY 2004

❧

IN THE SPANIARD'S BED
Helen Bianchin

MISTRESS BY AGREEMENT
Helen Brooks

THE LATIN LOVER'S SECRET CHILD
Jane Porter

THE UNCONVENTIONAL BRIDE
Lindsay Armstrong

A PAPER MARRIAGE
Jessica Steele

THE BILLIONAIRE TAKES A BRIDE
Liz Fielding

A WHIRLWIND ENGAGEMENT
Jessica Hart

THEIR MIRACLE BABY
Jodi Dawson

MILLS & BOON®

Live the emotion